*Fernhurst, Q.E.D., and*

*Other Early Writings*

*Fernhurst, Q.E.D., and*

*Other Early Writings*

GERTRUDE STEIN

LIVERIGHT  NEW YORK

"The Making of *The Making of Americans*," by Donald Gallup, copyright© 1950 by Duschnes Crawford, Inc., New York. Reprinted by permission.

*The publishers would like to thank the Estate of Gertrude Stein, and the Gertrude Stein Collection, Collection of American Literature, Beinecke Rare Book and Manuscript Library, Yale University for their invaluable and generous assistance.*

ISBN: 0-87140-082-0 (paper)
ISBN: 0-87140-532-6 (cloth)
Library of Congress Catalog Card Number: 71-148663

LIVERIGHT PAPERBOUND EDITION 1973

Manufactured in the United States of America

# Contents

# A Note on the Texts

*Fernhurst (1904-1905?):* The manuscript is written in ink on both sides of eighty-five leaves of a French school notebook (measuring 8-5/8 by 6-3/4 inches), with blank pages (in one case a leaf) before each new section of the work. The original title seems to have been "Fernhurst," then "The History of Philip Redfern, a Student of the Nature of Woman," and finally the present arrangement of title and subtitle. Some revision in ink and in pencil appears to have been made soon after the story was written, with extensive revision in pencil (in 1909?) when the story was incorporated, as the twenty-sixth of ninety-five notebooks, into the first full-length draft of *The Making of Americans.* At that time, six and one-half pages at the beginning of the manuscript, the greater part of twelve pages at the end, and some other shorter passages were omitted, and names and tenses changed throughout. Thirty leaves (which may well have been blank) were excised from the end of the notebook. Notes concerning the use of the old story in the new work appear here and there in the text and on the verso of the free front and the recto of the free back endpaper. For this present edition the original version has been reconstructed by ignoring all the obviously late changes. (For the revised text see pages 429–440 and 445 of *The Making of Americans* as published by Contact Editions in Paris in 1925 and reprinted by offset by the Something Else Press in New York in 1965).

*Q.E.D. (1903):* The manuscript, bearing the title "Quod Erat Demonstrandum," is written in ink on the rectos of the leaves (with the exceptional use of a few versos) in two French school notebooks (measuring 8-3/4 by 7 inches), with some later, slight revision in pencil. For an account of the circumstances under which Gertrude Stein came across this manuscript in the spring of 1932, see page 104 of her *The Autobiography of Alice B. Toklas* as published in New York by Harcourt, Brace and Company in 1933. The notebooks were sent by Alice B. Toklas to Carl Van Vechten, Miss Stein's literary executor, in 1947, and Mr. Van Vechten presented them to the Yale Library on behalf of Miss Toklas in 1950. The manuscript, with some changes of names and phrases, was printed in a limited edition (516 copies) in 1950 by the Banyan Press, Pawlet, Vermont, with the title *Things As They Are*. In the present version, Miss Stein's original text has been restored.

*The Making of Americans (1903):* The manuscript is written in ink on both sides of thirty-six leaves of a legal-size English notebook (measuring 12-1/2 by 8-1/4 inches), as described by Leon Katz in his introduction. Three leaves excised between the title leaf and what is now the beginning of the text indicate that some other introductory material may have been deleted. There is some, mostly minor, revision both in ink and in pencil. About thirty-nine leaves have been excised from the end. The notebook was included by Miss Stein with the manuscripts deposited through Thornton Wilder in the Yale Library in 1937, and was given to the Library with the rest of the deposited material in 1945.

*Editorial method:* In the transcription of all three texts, spelling errors ("akward," "dissaproved," "fullfill," etc.) and obvious slips of the pen have been silently corrected except that the characteristic Stein spelling "alright" for "all right" has been retained. Missing question marks throughout *Q.E.D.* and a few other punctuation marks that seemed necessary for ease of reading have been supplied; otherwise the punctuation is Miss Stein's.

DONALD GALLUP

# Introduction

## by Leon Katz

THE THREE WRITINGS issued in this volume—two for the first time and the longer *Q.E.D.* in a corrected edition—represent the first steps of Gertrude Stein's literary progress. In them lie the beginnings of her gradually articulated attack on the single problem at which she labored—with passion, with dedication, with monotonous persistence—until 1911, when she finished her mammoth family novel, *The Making of Americans:* the problem of describing the "last touch" of human being, or to put it another way, of passing beyond the practical acquaintance with human being which anyone can have to a total description of human being such as no one before her had dreamed of formulating. Her focus on this intention gained momentum and assurance through the first years of her writing life—from 1903 when she set down the first chapters of what was intended to be the conventional story of an American family's progress and decay to 1908 when, totally committed to her extraordinarily intense

vision of human psychology, she began to channel all the
matter of her book *The Making of Americans* into a massive
description of the psychological landscape of human being
in its totality.

With the exception of *Q.E.D.*, the writings collected in
this volume are apprentice work, but through them lies the
way to an understanding of one of this century's most original creative innovators. The inherent logic of Stein's work,
probably more than that of any other writer of our time, has
to be understood by recovering its chronology. It was her
habit throughout her writing life to return again and again
to her simplest and most direct human observations, and to
reformulate, in successive waves so to speak, the fundamental objective of writing itself. The increment of each previous
attempt, the residue of each formulation, was retained as
tested and true. And the increment of each writing period
set the direction for the next. The peculiar combination of
nervous vitality and stupefying inertia discernible in her
writing career comes from these successive lunges and returns to her root problems—what is writing? what is knowing? what is describing?—and from her successive methods
for finding and testing the answers.

The story of her commitment to psychological exploration and of her final bleak image of human relations is at
bottom the story of an obsessive personal yearning for explanation. The very obsessiveness of her curiosity charged
her crabbed and formulistic psychological ruminations
finally with almost visionary intensity. The story begins,
aptly enough, with an affair which was to serve as Stein's
paradigm for the underlying struggle and the maddening
obfuscation at the bottom of all human relations.

Before Stein left America in 1903 for her permanent stay in Europe, she had been living through an agonizing love affair which is recounted in minute and accurate detail in *Q.E.D.,* her first completed novel. This affair with a fellow-student at Johns Hopkins, May Bookstaver, had been following a complicated and desperate course not only because of a rival, but also because of the frustration of trying to fathom the woman she loved, and the impossibility of ever knowing whether May Bookstaver loved her in return, or was capable of loving at all. The affair was to end a year later with a moan and a whimper, but it was years before the effects of its torment wore off. These years with May marked the decline of Stein's assertive naiveté about herself and the beginning of her somber psychological wisdom. Through the long misery of the affair Stein suffered a series of insights concerning human conflict which lay at the bottom of all her subsequent psychologizing.

Their friendship started during Stein's last year as a regular student at Hopkins. While her brother Leo was in residence, they shared a flat, Leo curled up reading history and Stein working away at a mess of experimental paraphernalia in her own room; but in other respects, they lived and thought as one. Their circle of friends had been largely the same, consisting of distant Baltimore cousins and fellow students. Both brother and sister saw most of their friends as living in various kinds of moral torpor, and both had their minds set on their reform.

Leo had attracted a circle of younger students, and was teaching them "to free themselves of all conventions." It seemed to Emma Lootz and Mabel Weeks, fellow-students of his and Gertrude's, an irresponsible way for him to find expression for his own sense of liberation, but his disciples were satisfied. "I have never forgotten you," one of them wrote to him ten years later, "for you made whatever there will be of me." Stein emulated her brother on a smaller scale and with less success. She did not deal with groups but with one at a time, and she did not contend with fledglings but with equals—adversaries rather than disciples. She bludgeoned Emma Lootz, sandbagged Marian Walker—both strong-minded and ready for fight. Leo's and Gertrude's techniques were different, but their object was the same: to operate radically on all their friends' vital ethical deficiencies.

During the first year Leo was away in Europe, Gertrude, continuing on her own their program of earnest reform, met a group of women students who had come from eastern colleges. They were bright and athletic women, all "activity and no dreaminess." They were not only fellow-students at medical school, but well-to-do and well-connected young women who were not so much rebelling as on holiday from their Quaker past. In the normal run of things, students in Stein's mediocre social position would have found no place among them, but among them she was, as everywhere else, accepted as an original. But they moved her to wrath.

The group was led by Mabel Haynes and Grace Lounsbury, both from Bryn Mawr, who shared quarters in Baltimore and gave teas at which the contingent of Hopkins students from Smith College would gather. Stein, unable to contain herself at one of these teas, suddenly barked out: "I've been trying to describe you Smith women to myself, and I've finally got it. Raw virginity!"

She was wrong. The rawness was hers, not theirs. She could not begin, when she first met them, to cope with their

sophisticated manoeuvering between understood truths and
spoken lies. And she was naive enough to mistake their
devious and controlled expression of emotions for emotional
repression. She was facing seasoned libertarians with nothing but her four-square moral pieties about ambiguous
American morality and liberating one's self from the traps
of convention.

Stein had no suspicion that Mabel Haynes, after dropping
her friendship with Miss Lounsbury, had now taken May
Bookstaver into a kind of protective custody, having arranged to pay her extra bills and to take her to Europe and
on trips to her own home in Boston. She was aware of nothing but the justice and propriety of weaning May Bookstaver
away from the "anaemic" Miss Haynes and her "unaspiring" circle.

But within a few weeks Stein found herself out of her
emotional depth. Privately, and uneasily, she confessed to
May—as she reports in *Q.E.D.*—that she had an almost
puritanical horror of "passion in its many disguised forms,"
that she understood it little and that it had no reality for
her. May told her bluntly that her ignorance was visible.
"That is what makes it possible for a face as thoughtful and
strongly built as yours to be almost annoyingly unlived."
Stein answered solemnly, "I could undertake to be an
efficient pupil if it were possible to find an efficient teacher."

In the description of this episode in *Q.E.D.*, Stein concludes the incident with a dignified hiatus: "And then they
left it there between them." In reality, when Stein asked for
instruction, May burst out laughing. And Stein for a long
time remembered her shock at being laughed at for her
innocence. And she remembered it as the first significant

step toward her genuine maturity. The revelation of her ignorance led to weeks of perpetual questioning and moral confusion, but not to decision. She allowed herself to "drift" into an ambiguous understanding with May—ambiguous in a double sense: Stein understood neither the language of sign and gesture that May was using nor the precise moral significance of what either of them was doing. Not talking the same language, neither could begin to understand what the other's genuine feeling was.

But in her literal way, Stein, now in love, charged into an intensive course of instruction in genuine passion. By the time she left for Europe to join Leo for the summer of 1901, she felt that she could count to her credit no more than a troubled "glimpse" into May's emotional world, but she was satisfied that she was not merely indulging herself "superficially." It was a temporary satisfaction. Again and again she was to have sudden illuminations of May's questionable seriousness—though these alternated with the conviction that it was greater than her own—and at these moments she would be overcome by the nauseating feeling that she had fallen into the merest sordidness, into "un-illumined" immorality.

In Tangiers and Granada she chanced to read the *Vita Nuova*, and she rejoiced, "At last I begin to see what Dante is talking about and so there is something in my glimpse and it's alright and worthwhile," and she went back to America in October refreshed for further instruction.

There was little else, in fact, that demanded her return. Before leaving, she had failed almost all her courses at medical school, which put an end to her student days at Hopkins. With nothing to do in Baltimore, but with nothing else to do in any other place, she returned in the fall of 1901, after a few weeks of visiting in New York, to the house she shared with Emma Lootz on East Eager Street, and settled down to a year of purposeless improvisation.

During the course of the year, as she lived doggedly through the increasingly entangling relations with May and Mabel Haynes, several notions emerged from her attempt to understand the hazy drives that governed May's behavior, and the increasingly astonishing depths out of which her own behaviour seemed to spring. This simple formula becomes one of the *leit-motifs* of the character analyses in *The Making of Americans:* the interplay of two or more whole "characters" in a single personality. On the model of her analysis of May, Stein in her novel begins her psychological descriptions by asserting her initial bewilderment, after which her fragmentary recognitions of her subjects' fundamental traits polarize into sets of discrete and often contradictory "selves"; then, after a regimen on Stein's part of intense listening and watching, the separate "persons" are observed to reintegrate. The drama of discovery is endlessly the same: character is opaque, then abstracted into an unrelated series of separate entities, then abstracted once again by an intuitive grasp of the unifying principle of the weird assortment of entities.

During the same interview with May, Stein fastened on another duality. "You," she told May, are "Anglo-Saxon, brave, passionate but not emotional, capable of great sacrifice but not tender-hearted." If she wants things badly enough, May goes out and gets them. But Stein, by contrast, wants things only in order to understand them, "and I never go and get them. I am a hopeless coward, I hate to risk

hurting myself or anybody else. All I want to do is to meditate endlessly and think and talk."

The contrast between them was to become the paradigm
for the contrast between all lovers in Stein's character system, attracting by opposition of type and function. One fights
by attacking, the other by sullen resistance. It is not yet true
in either *Q.E.D.* or "Melanctha," the first two works based
on the "understanding" of the affair with May, that love,
friendship, even conversation are viewed as fundamentally
naked struggles for dominance and power, but characters in
all the early works are arranged in contrasting pairs and
triads, and the early stories are dramas of how difference
and misunderstanding overlap and blur with accord and
recognition. The contrast between kinds of character—the
one with respect to which all other contrasts are subordinate
—remained essentially an elaboration of the one introduced
here: a "clean," "Anglo-Saxon," courageously attacking
Siegfried opposes a "dirty," "earthy," cowardly Alberich,
sullenly defending his treasure at the mouth of his filthy
cave. The Siegfried prototype tends to be superficial in his
examination of himself, and, acting from a sense of his own
courageous strength and cleanliness, rarely knows that he is
even capable of lying; the Alberich, sunk in the mud of his
own cowardly indolence, lives familiarly with the world of
lies as well as with the grim knowledge of all his imperfections.

During the remainder of the winter, Mabel Haynes deftly
pursued her advantage by further revelations, and Stein
found herself engaged in a struggle between reverence for
one May and intense revulsion of feeling for the other. But
she had gone a long way toward the winning of wisdom. In

answer to one of May's embittered and contemptuous charges that Stein was trampling "everything ruthlessly under your feet . . . without being changed or influenced by what you so brutally destroy," Stein begged for patience. "It is hardly to be expected that such a changed estimate of values, such a complete departure from established convictions as I have lately undergone could take place without many revulsions."

The year in America ended with quarrels about Mabel Haynes, and with May's reiterated protests against Stein's "brutality." Stein sailed for Europe in the spring of 1902 to join Leo again, even less resolved and less certain than she had been the year before.

Realizing that it would take much time and strength to let all these complexities settle again, Stein planned to stay in Europe for a year, keeping close to May only through correspondence. Her resolve held firm through her stay with Leo in Florence and Haslemere, where Bernard Berenson's circle served as effectual distraction, but after a summer of pleasurably violent quarreling with Berenson and his friends, brother and sister removed to London, where Stein eased into morbid depression. The five months in London, where they lived in Bloomsbury—among the blackest of Stein's memories—were spent in lonely misery after Leo's sudden departure for Paris in December.

In a sense, *The Making of Americans* was begun during these months in England in 1902. Though not a word of the book was written then, she started keeping the notebooks which gradually accumulated the memories, observations, quotations, and story material which were to be the matter of the book.

Stein's solace during her enforced loneliness after Leo's departure was the British Museum. Living in its shadow, she would arrive at the reading room early in the morning and read until late at night, leaving only when she was hungry. When she was off this regimen, she wandered the dismal London streets. "Anything can frighten her and London when it was like Dickens certainly did."

Her reading at the Museum and from Mudie's bookstore was done with a rough plan in mind: to read through English narrative writing from the sixteenth century to the present. She bought a set of minute grey-covered notebooks in which she entered her lists for reading and buying books, and into which she copied passages for the pleasure of having them.

This reading program never halted throughout the years of her writing of the novel. The notebooks' lists are made up of books of any date, but as the years go on, the bulk of her reading moves generally from the fifteenth and sixteenth centuries to the nineteenth. The most striking fact about these lists is that not a single volume of criticism, philosophy, essays, poetry, or drama appears on them. There are several hundred titles set down in all, and with occasional exceptions such as the Spanish *Lazarillo de Tormes,* the *Arabian Nights,* George Sand memoirs, Russian novels, or anthologies of Oriental tales, they are made up entirely of major, minor, and very minor English novels and collections of tales; of diaries, letters, biographies, and autobiographies; and compendious volumes of history like Clarendon's and Gibbon's. There is an illuminating suggestion in this exclusiveness of her reading interest in narrative. Her feeling for the long roll of events was formed by long reading habit and from her peculiar experience of English narrative tradition. Nowhere in the notebooks is there any discussion of form or style. She "settled" into her style; its originality was the inadvertent consequence of trying to describe relations and events synoptically without losing traditional narrative's feel for the thick flow of time.

After five miserable months of loneliness and depression, the London winter proved too much to bear, and Stein was honest enough to confess that she was returning to America not for May's sake but for the sake of cleanliness and simplicity. She left for America in February of 1903. For a while she rejoiced in New York, in snow, in the realization that all its tall, straight, undecorated buildings were "without mystery and without complexity." But soon she was immersed in the interrupted affair, which was considerably more depressing than London's smoke.

In the weeks that followed her return, that portion of her drama with May was enacted which gave Stein her greatest insight into human relations—one which was to remain the key to her whole clumsy systematization of psychology, and one which would largely redeem the dull, opaque abstraction on which her speculations on character might have altogether foundered.

"We have just gotten into position," Stein announced to May after a few more weeks of emotional skirmishing between them. It was profoundly true. Stein finally reached the stage of feeling toward which May had been beckoning her all along, and giving up all worries about the moral ambiguities and the alternate meanings of their acts and words, with nothing of their former problems resolved but merely by-passed, Stein, feeling she had reached "perfect happiness," surrendered to the tides of impulse and feeling that allowed her to accept without doubts or lingering hesitation the efficient teacher she had asked May to be at the very start of their grim affair. The terrain of which Stein had caught a mere "glimpse" at the very beginning had finally become her daily habitation.

But "we have just gotten into position." From now on, it was no longer possible for Stein to pretend that the difference between them lay in their conflicting "values" or their differing experience; conflict of that kind lay behind them. And yet gradually they reached the same emotional impasse in which they had found themselves many times before. But their failure now seemed to stem from a kind of inevitable internal machinery that governed each one's responses and acts. In essence, it was a matter of timing. Beyond all other differences that destroyed their harmony was the difference, as Stein put it later, in the "rhythms" of their personalities: "Their pulses were differently timed." On reflection, it was possible to discern the same pattern of "difference" between them from the very beginning: the difference in their experience had reflected it; their ways of arguing had reflected it; as had even the characteristic way in which each had arrived at understandings and decisions in the course of their affair.

Stein remained convinced of the profound reality of this troubled insight of hers into human existence, and used it for the climactic episode in her recountings of the affair with May, in both *Q.E.D.* and "Melanctha." In *The Making of Americans*, the concept was reborn in new and more elaborate guises. But it was not until the writing of the final chapter of the novel, in 1911, that her insight was fully—and magnificently—implemented in her description of the continuous rhythmic pattern of David Hersland's life from the beginning of his self-consciousness until his death.

While the affair with May was following its last downward swing into hopeless impasse, Stein was quartered in New York in an apartment building called the White House, on 100th Street and Riverside Drive, and in a desultory way, continued the reading program and note-taking she had started in London. Though her program of going through English narrative writing bore signs of efficiency and energy, her reading habits did not, and during her last year in Baltimore and in New York, when any kind of sequential activity was a bother to her, every vestige of studious application was lost. She would sit down with a volume, thumb a few pages, read for some minutes on end, and then fall to thinking tangential thoughts which absorbed her more than her reading did.

Her speculations, like her later writing, were rapid, notions flashed quickly before her, and she would start putting them to imaginary use in the process of reading. One must remember that though prodigious portions of her time were spent in reading, she was influenced by few writers—and even by these, in only small ways—as one understands "influence" of ideas and style. Hints from other writers were taken in by a sort of ingestion, and even then, only if they entered smoothly into the strong drift of her own beliefs and predilections, for she read, as she listened, with absorbed inattention.

Between meetings with May and conscientious stock-taking of her emotions, there were long periods of bored indolence at the White House. She shared her flat with three friends, all of whom had been at Hopkins with her: Harriet

Clark, Estelle Rumbold, and Mabel Weeks. She spent her time sprawled in a chair in her room reading or ruminating, then stopping into one of the others' rooms for a talk, then wandering down to meals. During these months when she was merely filling time, she started a novel about a family.

At least, so it seems. Since it has been generally assumed that *The Making of Americans* was started in Paris in April of 1906, the evidence for its having been begun in New York three years earlier must be spelled out.

The notes written in 1906 for the novel are very clearly plans for revising old material, not for starting a new book. They consider addenda and rearrangements of an earlier text, and include brief notations such as, "begin this the other end to from my old book." The manuscript of the first five chapters of the "old book," from which the text of the first draft printed in this volume is taken, is set down in a large (legal-size) bound notebook whose end leaves are stamped with the trademark: "The English Manufactory of Book and Register." The top left-hand corner of the inside cover is price-marked in pencil: 2/9½. There is also extant a typed version of the fifth chapter of this "old book" which incorporates a few corrections of the manuscript.

Since Stein did not return to England for some years after 1902, the notebook was evidently bought there before February of 1903. When were the chapters in it written? In the apostrophe to the "public" which opens the second chapter, Stein writes: "I am strong to declare even here in the heart of individualistic America. . . ." In the published version, the same apostrophe is included, but is revised to read: ". . . here in the heart of this high, aspiring, excitement loving people. . . ." and the paragraph's address to "brother Americans" is altogether deleted. Since Stein left America in the spring of 1903, the only time she could have been writing the first version of the book in "individualistic America" was during her stay at the White House in New York.

The beginning of *The Making of Americans,* then, precedes not only *Three Lives* but her supposed first novel, *Q.E.D.,* as well. The "old book" represents the very first stage of her ambition to become a serious writer, if one discounts the novel she had started as a student at Radcliffe, a college story of adolescent struggle. The first draft of *The Making of Americans* then was written during the last desperate months of uncertainty with May Bookstaver. The quotation from Lyly's *Euphues,* which she had copied out in London and echoed in the planned last paragraph of the first draft, and the compendious list of English narratives which she had written out in London and in New York during the winter support this supposition: Stein was seeking models in them for novel-writing and for a style.

She betrayed her models. Her style is both archaic and immature. It echoes directly, though in a softened and naive way, the archaisms of *Euphues,* which she was still reading. There is a perpetual dialogue with "my reader . . . if indeed there be any such"—which attempts to catch the courteous self-effacement of Lyly's conversational narrators and results in pontifical and awkward turns of phrase that barely begin to express the warm and sensible observations Stein was already capable of making. There is a striking difference between the homespun good sense of what she is saying and her artificially rhetorical way of saying it.

At most, only half the text of this "old book" is extant.

Before the end of the fifth chapter, the manuscript comes to an end. The rest of the leaves written on in the notebook—about the same number as still remain—are sliced out. From the notes on revision done three years later, it is clear that all that was to be used for the second draft were the pages that still remain; the continuation of the story beyond chapter five was discarded.

But from the extant text alone, it is evident that the original plan of the novel concerned a single family, not two as in the final version, and that "the decent family's progress" which Stein was going to narrate was that of the less important family of the finished book, the Dehnings. The novel was to be the record of the New York Steins, and most especially of their eldest daughter, Bird Stein, who was Gertrude's cousin, and it was to center on the story of her unhappy marriage to Louis Sternberger. And the moral of the story was an astonishingly conventional one: the headstrong Julia's fatal error in marrying an attractive bounder is a warning to daughters of solid bourgeois families, brought up in the "straitened bond" of solid middle-class family feeling and upright values, not to seek the excitements of the unknown, not to succumb to the attraction of choosing dangerously. Three years later the moral was to be expunged, and the implication of the story was to be reversed; but the change occurred after Stein's feelings about her cousin Bird and her family had themselves undergone bitter reversal.

But even when she was writing the book in New York, and deploring Julia's straying from the middle class "bond," Stein was writing not from the point of view of the bourgeois family but from the point of view of the bounder's anti-bourgeois "singularity." Her baldly conventional moral stemmed from a point of view that was intended to be so unconventional that it returned to, and found its most exact expression in, the essence of conventionality. The tragedy of Julia's marriage, Stein considered, came from her incapacity to understand the difference between superficial singularity and "passionate" singularity, and from the parallel failure on her husband's part to be genuinely "queer." Their trouble was a common American trouble, the same one Stein had preached about to May's and Mabel Haynes' set in Baltimore. America was still too young to produce a genuine class of morally elite, and therefore satisfied itself with thin imitations of types. Whether the type was the virtuous *bon bourgeois* or the vicious aristocrat or, best of all, the nobly "singular," the American had neither the easy habit nor the frank passion to commit himself to it wholly.

Stein scoffed at the bourgeois and the aristocrats who could not bring themselves to be themselves wholly, but mourned the failure of her own type, the noble breed who have the courage to go their singular way, to produce more genuine examples of themselves, or to win acceptance for what they were in the American community.

> Brother Singulars we are misplaced in a generation that knows not Joseph. We flee before the disapproval of our cousins, the courageous condescension of our friends who gallantly agree to sometimes walk the streets with us. . . .

and concluded that the only thing for her Brothers Singular to do was to give up the attempt and go back to Europe's bosom, from whence they all came in the first place.

. . . We fly to the kindly comfort of an older world accustomed to take all manner of strange forms into its bosom and
we leave our noble order to be known under such forms as that
of Henry Hersland [Julia's husband], a poor thing and hardly
even then our own.

The contempt Stein feels for "the poor thing" Henry
Hersland and his unimpressive showing as a "singular" type
is not visited on Julia, who was almost equally unimpressive
as a bourgeoise hankering for the flavor of the unusual.
Stein admires her heroine's courage; not her courage in being true to type, but in rushing with indomitable energy and
decision into her tragically inappropriate marriage. Stein
describes the long struggle between Julia and her patient,
admiring father, in which she eventually succeeds in asserting her "power of domination" over his opposition, and her
triumphant progress in sweeping aside all other opposition.
At this point, the drama of the Dehning daughters com-
mences: the drama of Julia's passionate, "agitated" misery
and that of her sister Bertha's empty, lifeless sorrow. Each
of them is caught in a bad marriage, and they respond in
opposite ways. And at this point too, Stein's genuine interest
in her story is ready to be exploited: the contrast in the
emotional life of two opposite bourgeois types. Contrast is
the key; the early pages of the new novel are clearly intended
to be a studied arrangement of "pairs" of characters in descriptive rather than in dramatic opposition to one another.

The first draft breaks off at the moment when Bertha finds
her proper suitor, a young man named Lohm, "the handsomest and biggest man in the most imposing bourgeois
family in their set," obviously a "contrast" to Julia's unreliable choice, Henry Hersland. Julia's first suspicion that

her future husband had a dark and unreliable side had already been stressed before Bertha's ostensibly satisfactory choice was introduced. The description of Bertha's parallel sorrow in marriage was sliced out of the manuscript and is lost, but that it was there can hardly be doubted. The method of the projected novel is set in the pages left, and the direction of Stein's first ten years of writing is already visible.

But most clearly visible is the difficulty into which she would run head-on: her commitment, as a conventional novelist, to narrative is fundamentally in opposition to her feeling for how character is to be observed and explained. She is in fact imagining human beings more in schematic than in active relations. Although "action" and narrative are among the possible avenues through which schematically conceived description of character can be made discernible, they do not properly set forth the full range of such observation. The gulf between telling a story in the usual sense and Stein's particular intent of making gradual revelation of whole natures is not new to her work, but the underlying contradiction between them becomes more and more explicit and troublesome in her writing until the technique of narrative altogether breaks down, and narration itself becomes submerged in a different sort of "composition."

That the difficulty was being felt by Stein herself when she was writing the first draft in New York is unlikely. When she returned to the novel after *Three Lives,* there is little question that her first order of business was to stop the "story" from running away with her essential reason for writing the book and that everything after the fifth chapter of the first version was thrown away so that her primary interest in writing the book could be explored further:

"Sense of human struggles," she notes, and then sets down all the character "struggles" she would like to use. But ambiguously enough, they turn out to be contrasts of two kinds: characters who actually "struggle" against one another, and characters in separate stories who are schematically opposed to one another. The first five chapters were held on to, and the succeeding story was to continue from the last page saved, because up to that point all the characters had in fact been arranged with respect to one another, and had already been so described. With a bit of pruning and touching up here and there, and with matter irrelevant to the new adventure in character description cut out, the first pages of the old New York writing were able to see service through the second draft.

But it was three years before she again took up the novel in earnest. When she sailed for Europe in the spring of 1903, the manuscript was put away, and until 1906 it was to be neither decisively discarded nor confidently resumed. Her plans for it, just as her plans for writing generally, were to remain, until after she wrote *Three Lives,* amorphous and ambiguous.

When Stein arrived in Paris, Leo had already started to set up house at 27 rue de Fleurus. She intended to stay for only a short time—perhaps through the winter—simply for the reason that she badly needed a holiday from the misery of her affair with May. She had even made arrangements for her return to New York in the spring almost as soon as she was settled with Leo in Paris. When she did return for several months to try for the last time to effect some kind of reconciliation with May, the attempt was abortive, and she settled in Paris for good.

The notebooks and her letters of the first months in Paris—
in fact of her first four years there—suggest that Stein under-
went a period of the most relentless despair, surrender of
ambition, and psychological disorientation. She became
passive, cynical; she was moved to do nothing. The picture
that she herself offers in her autobiographies of an eager,
not to say bouncing, enthusiast for Parisian art, for friends,
for her new life, was written from the happily distant perspective of the 1930s.

A trip to Italy in the summer was intended for con-
valescence. With Leo she went to Rome, but the drama
with May and Mabel pursued her there. The two of them
appeared one day on the Via Nazionale, and Stein at the
first moment was delighted to see them. But after a few days
of constant meeting, the tensions of their unspoken situation
began to tell on them all. Their meetings in Rome ended
with May worn and depressed and Stein "sad with longing
and sick with desire." She and May agreed secretly to meet
again in Florence or in Siena, where Stein was to be with the
most balanced and stabilizing of her "White House" friends,
Mabel Weeks.

In Siena Stein finally met Miss Weeks, who was to be her
walking companion. She took the opportunity to pour all her
perplexity, unhappiness, and complex self-justification into
Mabel Weeks's ear. Miss Weeks in later years remembered
this Gertrude, during their walking trip, as the most sorrowful and debilitated Gertrude she was ever to know. For
hours she poured out "Oscar Wildean justifications" for
the tangle into which she had fallen. The joyous, over-
whelmingly confident Stein of Hopkins days had altogether
disappeared.

When finally her friends left for America, Stein retired from the scene of her emotional disasters to the summer home of Hutchins Hapgood in the chestnut woods of Bagni di Lucca above Florence. Hapgood recalled that Stein's visit merged with the "quiet flow of peace and beauty" of the summer routine in the Florence hills, "and indeed that she didn't interfere with the flow." Hutchins had no reason to realize it, but Stein's passivity, new and strange for her, emanating as it did from three years of emotional trials and failure, was to stay with her for some years to come.

She shared her sorrows with none of her new friends in Europe. Apart from the intimate women friends in America with whom she corresponded, confiding in torrential out-bursts of indignation and subtle justification her feelings about her doomed love affair and from whom she demanded detailed news of the facts concerning the leading characters with whom she no longer corresponded, she veiled her most intimate feelings from everyone around her.

At the end of the summer Leo and Gertrude began their permanent residence in Paris at their rue de Fleurus flat. A few weeks after settling in, Stein wrote her last letter to May. "I almost wish sometimes," she wrote, "that you did not trust me so completely because then I might have some influence with you for now as you know you have my faith quite absolutely and as that is to you abundantly satisfying I lose all power of coming near you." May replied, begging her not to destroy the effect of her patient endurance all summer and assured Stein, as ambiguously and noncommit-tally as ever, that such conditions could hardly arise again. Stein read the letter impatiently. "Hasn't she yet learned that things do happen and she isn't big enough to stave them off. . . . Can't she see things as they are and not as she would make them if she were strong enough as she plainly isn't.

"I am afraid it comes very near being a deadlock," she groaned dropping her head on her arms.

Having finally seen "things as they are" herself, Stein settled into enduring the pain of her frustration for good, and ended abruptly all attempts to effect reconciliation with May.

All but one attempt. As she had done in the first ineffectual chapters of the family novel written in New York, Stein turned to writing to clarify the geometry of her situation. She pulled out all of May's letters and copies of her own, changed the names of the three women involved, and wrote out the whole story literally as it happened. For May she used the name Helen Thomas, after Helen Carey Thomas, the president of Bryn Mawr who was to figure importantly in one of the central episodes of *The Making of Americans*. For Mabel Haynes she chose the name Mabel Neathe, after Neith Boyce, Hutchins Hapgood's wife, whom she had just been visiting in Florence.

There was a more immediate reason for the association of Miss Thomas and Mabel. Alfred Hodder, an aberrant but radiant friend of the Harvard-Florence literary circle— a friend of Leo's, Hutchins Hapgood's, Bernard Berenson's and Gertrude's—had been teaching at Bryn Mawr with Mary Gwinn until 1898 while Carey Thomas was dean, and now, after six years of tantalizing and gossip-ridden adventure, he was preparing to divorce his wife and marry Miss Gwinn during the following summer in Paris. Stein, like all members of this group, had followed the scandal of Hodder's adventures over the years and was as intrigued as any of them by its possible outcome. Hodder's affair with Miss Gwinn had started in circumstances strikingly similar to those of Gertrude's own adventures: Hodder and Miss Gwinn were in the position Gertrude and May had been in, with Carey Thomas making up the third member of a triangle just as Mabel Haynes had done.

About a year after the completion of *Q.E.D.* in October of 1903, Stein undertook a second fictional exploration of the puzzling questions of power and policy in love, and wrote an independent fictional episode based on the Hodder affair called *Fernhurst*. The study ended up in the pages of *The Making of Americans*. By that time it had been revised in the light of Stein's later psychological vocabulary, but enough of the piece was left in its original form to make clear its tangible connection with events at Bryn Mawr.

Hodder was first known to Gertrude and Leo as one of Harvard's most brilliant graduate students in philosophy. Leo, in fact, thought so highly of his philosophic acumen that, during his first year alone in Europe when he was going through his perennial crisis concerning his vocation, he wrote to Gertrude that Hodder's doctoral thesis, *The Adversaries of a Skeptic,* had turned his attention again to metaphysics "for it suggested the only path in which I can walk in comfort. If I find that it breaks down I think that I shall be able to drop metaphysics for good." The thesis had already had the same effect on Hodder who, after finishing it, acquired contempt for the academic life. Diffidently, almost for the fun of it, Hodder accepted a job teaching philosophy at Bryn Mawr. Although William James had recommended him, Josiah Royce, who had known him as an undergraduate and had felt that he was the most promising student of philosophy ever graduated from the University, thought nevertheless "that his usefulness as a philosopher might be sadly damaged if not entirely destroyed by his romantic temperament." It was. Hodder arrived at Bryn Mawr with a wife and children. "Clever, unstable, a good talker, experienced in the ways of women," he flattered Miss Gwinn with both his courtly and intellectual attentions. And Miss Gwinn, "who had hitherto arrogantly eschewed acquaintance with any man," succumbed.

No one could have anticipated Miss Gwinn's surrender. For years, she had been living in the shadow of Bryn Mawr's ambitious, almost ruthless, and brilliant dean. For Miss Thomas this association had meant everything. As an educator she had formed Miss Gwinn's intellect; as a leading fighter in the cause of women's rights she had formed Miss Gwinn's beliefs in the value of women's independence and scholarly pursuits. Miss Gwinn had been a brilliant lecturer in her own right, famous throughout the college as the teacher who had "set the tone of Bryn Mawr's intellectual life." Nevertheless she had always been an "enigmatic figure" at the college, "both repellent and fascinating: dark haired, dark eyed, white skinned, tall, elegant; physically indolent, languid in movement, studied in gesture; selfish, sometimes malicious; and mentally, brilliantly, subtly active."

In telling their story, Stein invested Miss Gwinn with May's psychological ambiguities and created a more aggressive version of Mabel Haynes in Carey Thomas. Hodder was given a peculiar association with Woodrow Wilson. Wilson had taught at Bryn Mawr under Miss Thomas' deanship and they had collided. The introverted, cold, and emotionally narrow Wilson was diametrically opposed to Miss Thomas's extroversion, masculine strength of purpose, and sense of superiority. With a southerner's old-fashioned ideals concerning women, he was offended by Miss Thomas's aggressive independence. Since the rivalry between them had been famous and had been in part responsible for Wilson's resignation from the college, Stein turned Hodder into the southerner, Philip Redfern, and modeled the collision of personality between the dean and Redfern on Wilson's difficulties with Carey Thomas.

The role she chose for her own portrait was that of Hodder's wife—a quiet, not too intelligent, intellectually helpless plodder who does not understand her husband's complexities, who supposes naively that her love for her husband will be sufficient to hold him and who becomes utterly confused and dully helpless when the affair with Miss Gwinn gets under way. It takes her months to understand precisely what her situation is, and she makes the discovery only through Miss Thomas's broad hint to her to keep an eye on her husband. This information leaves her even more helpless and bewildered than she had been when she had not suspected anything. In a leaden way, she undergoes several days of moral self-questioning on the problem of how much right she has to confront her husband with his misdemeanor or even to inquire into it. Finally she makes up her mind. She pulls a letter from his desk, opens it and reads a message from Miss Gwinn. Stein concluded the episode with a kind of melodramatic second-act curtain. "She read it to the end, she had her evidence."

Luckily the writing of the Hodder episode went no further. As writing and as story-telling it was young. But clearly Stein was attracted to the question of Hodder's relation to three women at this moment of his life because of its striking parallels to her own situation and because it offered her still another opportunity to "geometrize" the relations of pairs and threes. For all the derivative prose of the episode, Carey Thomas, for example, is still psychologically partitioned into separate and distinct categories of response and motive. Miss Gwinn is given May's aura of ambiguity with the addition of her own brilliance and poise, and the old power struggle in love relationships is repeated.

It is impossible to think of Stein adapting herself to the negative role of Mrs. Hodder at any other time of her life. All her feelings of self-doubt—her certainty that she is stupid, that she is morally rigid, that she is last among all women—emerges in this portrait. When in 1909—five years later—this whole episode, written independently of any other work, was incorporated whole into *The Making of Americans,* Stein used it as the climactic episode for the story of Martha Hersland, who of the three Hersland children is the dullest, the emptiest, and the least successful. But by 1909 she had sufficiently recovered from her troubles to divorce herself from the character of Martha and from Mrs. Hodder's role in the episode. They were attached at that time to several other women who, in the psychological pantheon Stein was currently constructing, fit more appropriately into the sorry category of which she had formerly thought herself the chief example.

According to Alice Toklas, Stein "wrote the Hodder story probably a year or so after it happened," but Miss Toklas was not clear about the date. "Gertrude said of this section in *The Making of Americans* that she took it complete from an isolated thing . . . but it was never rewritten. That is why there is such a break in tone and style" between this section and the rest of the novel.

The "break in tone and style" is violent. Stein stuck to her resolve to include the "Fernhurst" sequence in the Martha chapter of *The Making of Americans,* but after faithfully copying it into the new manuscript, she found herself shocked at the emptiness of its prose style. Instead of throwing it away and rewriting it in her new, far more authentic, and personal style, she appended an embarrassed editorial note to the passage, and followed her editorial paragraph with a complete rewriting of the episode in her current manner. The apologetic paragraph provides an illuminating commentary on the progress she had made toward finding her own writer's voice in the five years between the writing of *Fernhurst* and the writing of the Martha Hersland chapter in the long novel:

Categories that once to someone had real meaning can later in that same one be all empty. It is queer that words that meant something in our thinking and feeling can later come to have in them in us not at all any meaning. . . . There is . . . so complete a changing of experiencing in feeling and thinking, . . . that something once alive to some one is then completely a stranger to that one, the meaning in a word to that one the meaning in a way of feeling and thinking that is a category to

some one, . . . these then come to be all lost to that one sometime later in the living of that one.

. . . some then have a little shame in them when they are
copying an old piece of writing where they are using words
that sometime had real meaning for them and now have not
any real meaning in them to the feeling and the thinking and
the imagining of such a one . . . . Often then I have to lose
words I have once been using, now I commence again with
words that have meaning, a little perhaps I had forgotten when
it came to copying the meaning in some of the words I have
just been writing. . . . now to begin a description of Philip
Redfern and always now I will be using words having in my
feeling, thinking, imagining very real meaning.

Hodder left Bryn Mawr with Miss Gwinn early in 1904;
during his trip through Europe, where he married Miss
Gwinn during the summer, he visited the rue de Fleurus,
and saw Hapgood in Italy. The writing of *Fernhurst* undoubtedly preceded *Three Lives* (begun in the spring of
1905), since after *Three Lives* was finished, *The Making of
Americans* was taken up at once. Late 1904 or early winter
of 1905, then, seem the only possible dates for the composition of the episode.

The three stories published here are all apprentice-pieces.
Stein's genuinely original work begins with her next composition, the extraordinary stories published in *Three Lives*.
It was during the writing of the longest of these stories,
"Melanctha," when Stein came under Cézanne's influence
and was sitting for her portrait by Picasso, that the novelty
of her art makes its first genuine appearance, and what she
accomplished in it as a writer did not escape her. It was

revolutionary in its method of narration and description; and its insight into the relation of the two lovers described was unique. Again, the same love affair is used as the paradigm for love: ostensibly the story of a mulatto girl and a Negro doctor in Baltimore, "Melanctha" is in fact the story of *Q.E.D.* in disguise, with May Bookstaver as Melanctha and Stein as the tormented doctor.

The moment the story was completed, she went back to the notes and the unskillful chapters for the family novel written three years before, and decided to write it after all, but this time developing in it what had found such strong expression in "Melanctha"; that is, her ability to sift through the complexities of personality and to observe and describe the interior history of these complexities as the characters circled through the orbit of their relationships. It was in "Melanctha" that Stein at last brought into focus, with a kind of dazzling quality and richness of texture, what had been present but largely dormant and thinly expressed in the first draft of the novel and in *Q.E.D.* And with the confidence born of its achievement, it was inevitable that the psychological dynamisms so strongly conceived in her first work would become articulated and adumbrated with obsessive zeal in the enormous landscape of human relations now being projected for the long novel.

Then, after years of fitful stops and starts, of disappointing setbacks, and critical months when the whole design and purpose of her unique work, not to say its justification, were blurred and lost to her, of outbursts of fury against her brother and both his friends and hers who warned her that her writing was becoming meaningless, monotonous, and childish—after five years of this dogged and irrational persistence—the last chapter of *The Making of Americans* was set down in less than a month, and was written in a torrential rush which spelled out with clarity, with control, with utter integrity, and with the most moving command of her fantastically complex and subtle material the inner life of her hero from the beginning of consciousness until death. After his death, the memory and the forgetting of him are described as moving into and "distributing" themselves among the streams of continuing life so that the sorrow of his troubled existence and the sorrow of his unhappy death to some extent share permanently in, and to some extent disappear forever from, the weave of existence.

In this culminating section of the book—the consummate artistic performance of the first period of her writing—Stein's portrait of her hero leaves behind all the psychological and descriptive scaffolding which had become so cumbersome. As she confessed in the previous chapter on which she had labored to no good end for a year and a half, all these descriptive terms and crossed and complexified categories cluttered her whole and direct vision of human being. In a style cleaned and denuded of all echoes and imitations of other writers' manners, using only words which bore the impress of her own discovery of their full meaning and of her own conviction of their pregnancy, the chapter moves, like a rolling river, to the great dirge over the death of David Hersland. "Dead is dead," it begins, and as the elongated rhythms of Stein's prose sing mournfully over the event of the death, the text, not mournfully, not somberly, but matter-of-factly, persuades us more and more, again and again, with mounting clarity and certainty, that what is so is so, that from the perspective from which she as a writer is now viewing people, relations and events, the prospect of life that is illuminated for her is being grasped in a synoptic vision that can only be expressed in all its fullness, in its final descriptive translation, as altogether untranslatable, as describing itself, as a series of statements of identity. As Joyce puts it: "What is is"; as Stein puts it, "Each one is one," and "Dead is dead," and "Anyone has come to be a dead one."

To share even piecemeal, fragmentarily, the scope and certainty of the vision with which *The Making of Americans* is concluded is, it appears to me, to begin to see the distinction that informs the life-work that followed this novel. After the novel was finished, the portentous subject, the effort to achieve the grand manner, even the terms of formal intellectual discourse are all discarded, and her writing settles into a life-long, smiling, personal pageantry of the nearby and the trivial. There are stops and starts, there are redefinitions of the writing problem, there persist the experimental games of worrying metaphysical terms to the limits of their endurance to discover how much of them remains usable after they have been shoved into their most ridiculous postures. All that activity happily continues for the rest of her life. But beneath all of it, informing it and giving it its inevitability, lies the settled and visionary certainty for which the struggle and the concluding achievement of *The Making of Americans* served as the springboard.

Subsequently, the vision grew, and enlarged on that of the novel. It is a vision, paradoxically, of the "literally true." The phrase is used as the title for one of her works, and it might be the title of all of them. It compares with the vision of certain mystics who lived with the compelling sense of total illumination, with all the parts of everything seen plainly, in unbroken and simple and easily perceived harmonies, the highest and the lowest together. Stein's vision had that clarity, that intensity, and that ease. She saw the reality of relations—at first, relations of people, then of objects in space, and then of events in time—with as much force and clarity as though they were tangible. The substance of what she saw—or to put it more accurately, the summary of it—was more or less profound or trivial or remarkable as different occasions for observation can be for anyone. But the tangibility of relations, for her, did not blur. There was nothing for her to say *about* them but that they were there; they were so, literally and tangibly true. In *Four Saints in Three Acts,* the saints having performed the last "act" that brings them to heaven and to the comfortable, at-home feeling with the Absolute that Stein felt with the literal, sing, as their final hosannah, not with strained ardor, but, so-to-speak, in the middle register of emotion: "Last Act. Which is a fact." They are there; everything is around them, and it is so, a fact. Rose, in the children's book, *The World Is Round,* has the same Steinian feeling. After the labor of climbing frightening mountain slopes carrying a chair with her, she gets to the top of the mountain, puts the chair down, and settles comfortably into it.

From that point of vantage—at which one is finished with the tentative, with the activity of arriving—all the shrillness of feeling, all the strain of conceptualizing, all the buttresses, in fact, needed to sustain incomplete, still-maturing understandings and conditions, disappear. For one like Stein, who is at home not with metaphysical or theological absolutes but with the commonly-so, with the literally-true, and whose main business is to write, that is, to convey—to be in *her* novel imaginative situation makes it inevitable that the buttresses and structures through which one normally reaches knowledge and through which one normally conveys it, will also fall away. The landscape of the intellect, the figurations of knowledge and the communication of it, flatten; their need, in their familiar forms, disintegrates.

When it is understood that this was Stein's imaginative condition, not her irresponsible invention; when the extraordinary point of vantage from which her insights, her concerns, her methods, her shifting styles emanated, is shared, it becomes plain that she was doing what every writer does: telling what she knew. She repeated this to the point of monotony: "I write what I know." She repeated it not because she was compulsive about repeating, but because nobody would believe that she meant it that simply, or in so usual a sense.

The writing of *The Making of Americans* then, and the fictions herein included and the notebooks which attended its writing, record Stein's struggle toward maturity and integrity of conviction as a person, as an observer, and as an artist. Germinating out of nine years of labor on fictional narratives which passed beyond the scope and limits of fictional form, from the settled center of her matured vision, out of the "flattening" of the hierarchies of thought and feeling which her intensity of vision finally achieved, her unique art subsequently emerged as an endlessly full hymn of pleasure in the actual, a nonselective tribute to the uniform splendors of existence.

LEON KATZ

# FERNHURST

*The History of Philip Redfern
A Student of the Nature of Woman*

A GUEST OF HONOR so custom demands begins an address with praise and humor and speaking to the ideals of the audience clothes the laudations in the technical language of the hearers' profession. It is known that post prandial attention must be fished with this bait and only slowly rises to interest and labor. So the selected bandar-log begins his imitating chatter with the praise of repetition and a learned lady delights her audience with a phrase and bids them rejoice in their imperfections. "We college women we are always college girls" she said and a few standing by reading a condemnation in these words of praise mocked in undertones at their deluded fellows.

The young woman of to-day up to the age of twenty one leads the same life as does her brother. She has a free athletic childhood and later goes to college and learns latin science and the higher mathematics. She in these days busies herself with sport and becomes famous on the ball-fields and in rowing and cricket, conducting herself in all things as if there were no sex and mankind made all alike and traditional differences mere variations of dress and contour.

I have seen college women years after graduation still embodying the type and accepting the standard of college girls—who were protected all their days from the struggles of the larger world and lived and died with the intellectual furniture obtained at their college—persisting to the end in their belief that their power was as a man's—and divested of superficial latin and cricket what was their standard but that of an ancient finishing school with courses in classics and liberty replacing the accomplishments of a lady. Much the same as a man's work if you like before he becomes a man but how much different from a man's work when manhood has once been attained.

I wonder will the new woman ever relearn the fundamental facts of sex. Will she not see that college standards are of little worth in actual labor.

I saw the other day a college woman resent being jostled by her male competitors in a rush for position—in spite of all training she was an American woman still, entitled to right and privileges and no more willing to adopt male standards in a struggle than her grandmother. She was neither less a woman or more dogged in battle though she had read latin and kicked a foot-ball.

Will different things never be recognised as different. I am for having women learn what they can but not to mistake learning for action nor to believe that a man's work is suited to them because they have mastered a boy's education. In short I would have the few women who must do a piece of the man's work but think that the great mass of the world's women should content themselves with attaining to womanhood.

There is a dean presiding over the college of Fernhurst in the state of New Jersey who in common with most of her generation believes wholly in this essential sameness of sex and who has devoted her life to the development of this doctrine in numerous pamphlets of her composition and in the implanting of this doctrine in the many students who attend her college. I have heard many graduates of this institution proclaim this doctrine of equality, with a mental reservation in favor of female superiority, mistaking quick intelligence and acquired knowledge for practical efficiency and a cultured appreciation for vital capacity and who valued more highly the talent of knowing about culture than the power of creating the prosperity of a nation.

This Dean of Fernhurst has had great influence in the lives of many women. She is possessed of a strong purpose and vast energy. She has an extraordinary instinct for the qualities of men and rarely fails to choose the best of the young teachers as they come from the universities. She rarely keeps them many years for either they attain such distinction that the great universities claim them or they are dismissed as not being able enough to be called away. The Dean of Fernhurst is hard headed, practical, unmoral in the sense that all values give place to expediency and she has a pure enthusiasm for the emancipation of women and a sensitive and mystic feeling for beauty and letters.

In accordance with the male ideal the college is governed by the students themselves in all matters relating to conduct but this government though in the hands of the students themselves is in truth wholly centred in the dean who dominated by a passion for absolute power administers an admirable system of espionage and influence which she interrupts with occasional bald exercise of authority and not infrequent ignominious retreats. This resolute and powerful personality gives the tone to the college and deeply influences all the students who attend it. Honorable and manly as are the ostensible ideals that govern the place the unmoral methods of the dean the doctrine of the superiority of woman and a sensitive and mystic appreciation of the more decadent forms of art are the more vital influences and many a graduate spends sorrowful years in learning in after-life that her quality is not more fine nor her power greater than that of many of her more simple fellows and that established virtues and methods are at once more honorable and more efficient.

What sentiment more admirable than devotion to one's alma mater. What influence in youth more delightful than that of college fellows. Such fond regard is felt by all sons of universities. But even in such simple devotion may lurk a danger and in different lives carry different meanings and women in a college of the same age in years as men are many years their elders in emotion, and treating as a life business this college experience receive an enduring stamp of their special college—then too their life does not immediately enlarge with the affairs of the big world and so put them out of conceit with their accepted standard. The colleges are various in their effect one college trains them to be cultured sophisticated perhaps decadent, another makes them aggressively healthy and crudely virgin, another increases their learning power at the expense of their health and appreciations and it has always seemed to me a dreadful task to de-

cide for any young woman, what college shall make for her
a character.

Toward Helen Thornton the Dean of Fernhurst, her
youth spent in a struggle to make women better—constant
of purpose—noble in aim ambitious for the welfare of her
race we the generation of women who have rights to refuse
should I suppose be silent and not bring the world to observe the contradiction in her doctrine and the danger of
her method. What! does a reform start hopeful and glorious
with a people to remake and all sex to destroy only to end
in the same old homes with the same men and women in
their very same place. Doctrines that have noble meanings
often prove in action futile. It is not without a kind of awe
and reverence that an observer should speculate on such
doctrines as he traces the course of them. I have seen too
much of successful reform to take off my hat and huzzah as
it appears triumphant in eulogy and would do my little best
with my complimenting neighbors that they should not ap-
plaud too loudly or fill their souls with too much hope. Is
it the Manchester school leading England to free-trade
philanthropy and prosperity or Joseph Chamberlain leading
them farther to protection selfishness and a great future. Is
it Susan B. Anthony clamoring for the increase of the suf-
frage or John Marshall pleading for its restriction, I gaze at
them and realise that the Manchester people and Chamberlain are alike desirous of England's glory and that Miss
Anthony and James Marshall are both eager that the truest
justice should be granted to all.

Had I been bred in the last generation full of hope and
unattainable desires I too would have declared that men and
women are born equal but being of this generation with the

college and professions open to me and able to learn that the other man is really stronger I say I will have none of it. And you shall have none of it says my reader tired of this posing, I don't say no I can only hope that I am one of those rare women that should since I find in my heart that I needs must.

WHEN PHILIP REDFERN had taken his doctor's degree in philosophy and presently after came to hold the chair of philosophy at Fernhurst college in the state of New Jersey the two very interesting personalities in the place were the dean Miss Thornton with her friend Miss Bruce the head of the department of English literature.

Redfern had previously had no experience of women's colleges but being a man deeply interested in the life of his time was not without theories and convictions concerning the values of this mode of existence and was prepared to make and find an experience with 500 intelligent women interesting and instructive. He knew something of the character of the dean of the place but had heard nothing of any other member of the institution and went to make his bow to his fellow instructors in some wonder of anticipation and excitement of mind.

The new professor of philosophy was invited by the Dean

to meet the assembled faculty at a tea at her house two days after his arrival in the place.

He entered alone and was met by the Dean, a dignified figure with a noble head and a preoccupied abrupt manner. She was somewhat lame and walked about leaning on a tortoise-shell stick the imperative movement of which made a way through all obstacles. "You must meet Miss Bruce" she said breaking rather rudely through the courtly politeness of the new instructor who was a Southerner and trained in elaborate chivalry, "She is our only other philosopher" and moving rapidly through the crowd she presented him to Miss Bruce.

Redfern looked with interest at this individual with whom he was to share the philosophic world and who appeared to him the most complete presentment of gentleness and intelligence that he had ever looked on. Her figure was tall thin and reserved, her face gentle and intelligent, her eyes shy and her fine waving hair tinged with grey, the whole embodying his mature ideal in a way that made his heart beat with surprise.

She greeted him with awkward shyness and after a few moments of stumbling effort to keep to formal talk she said abruptly "What is it that you really mean by naive realism" referring to a doctrine that he had voiced in a recent article. Redfern was surprised and amused and plunged gayly into abstruse metaphysics watching her the while with growing admiration.

Her talk was serious eager and intense, her point of view clear, her arguments just and her opinions sensitive. Her self consciousness disappeared during this eager discussion but her manner did not lose its awkward restraint, her voice its gentleness or her eyes their shyness. Redfern who had never before seen such fine intelligence combined with perfect gentleness felt that he was in the presence of that ideal that he had dreamed of but had not hoped to meet in this two sexed world and he listened to her with charmed attention bending toward her his tall clean built American body with its intelligent head, with its smooth shaven face, worn complexion and observant eyes.

To the last hour of Redfern's life he remembered her as she then looked and spoke, the long delicate fluttering fingers, the awkward reserved body, the gentle worn face and shy eyes.

While the pair were still in the height of discussion there came up to them a blonde eager good-looking young woman whom Redfern observing greeted with scrupulous courtesy and presented as his wife to his new acquaintance. Miss Bruce checked in her talk was thrown back into even more than her original shy awkwardness and looking with distress at this new arrival after several efforts to bring her mind to understand stammered out, "Mrs. Redfern yes yes of course your wife I had forgotten." She made another attempt to begin to speak and then suddenly giving it up gazed at them quite helpless.

"You were discussing naive realism" said Mrs. Redfern nervously, "pray go on I am very anxious to hear what you think of it," and Redfern bowing to his wife with his scrupulous courtesy turned again to Miss Bruce and went on with his talk and soon Miss Bruce was again lost in the full tide of metaphysics and oblivious of all small human perplexities.

An observer would have found it difficult to tell from the

mere appearance of this trio what their relation toward each other was. Miss Bruce was absorbed in her talk and thought and oblivious of everything except discussion, her shy eyes fixed on Redfern's face and her tall constrained body filled with eagerness, Redfern was listening and answering with alternating argument and epigram, showing the same degree of courteous deference to both his companions, his intelligent face with its square forehead, long vigorous chin, worn complexion, firm mouth and observant eyes turned first toward one and then toward the other with impartial attention and Mrs. Redfern nervous and uneasy, her blonde good-looking face filled with eager anxiety to understand listened to one and then the other with the same anxious care. It was a group that would have puzzled the most practiced of interpreters.

Finally the friend with whom Mrs. Redfern had entered the room made her way up to them and others joining naive realism was dropped and the talk became general. The group shortly broke up and they moved about drinking tea, making epigrams, talking of college matters, and analysing Swinburne, Oscar Wilde and Henry James, each one anxious to meet the new instructor whom you may be sure they were all observing, praising and condemning and who moved about among them brilliant in talk gay and friendly in manner with his exact Southern courtesy, keen intelligent face and observant eyes.

At last sufficient tea had been drunk every one had been met and an amazing number of epigrams had been made and Redfern wandered up to a window where the Dean Miss Bruce and Mrs. Redfern were standing looking out at a fine prospect of sunset and a long line of elms defining a road that led back through the village of Fernhurst through the wooded hills behind, purple in the sunset and beautiful to look at. Redfern stood with them looking out at the scene.

———————    ———————    ———————*

said Miss Bruce quoting the lines from the *Iliad*. Mrs. Redfern listened intently, "Ah of course you know Greek" she said with eager admiration. Miss Bruce made no reply and the Dean began to describe to the new comers what lay before them and what she always loved to dwell on namely the history of the place. How twenty years ago she was at a friend's house at Richmond and how there one day she described the struggles of a young woman who was trying to educate herself in the higher mathematics and how a wealthy Richmond woman who was present became interested in the matter and gradually became convinced that there should be the same work for men and women and how this college with Miss Thornton as Dean had been founded fifteen years ago as the result of this chance meeting. "And now" concluded Miss Thornton "it is no longer an experiment, the equal capacity of women and men has been perfectly shown." Redfern to whom this last remark was addressed bowed and assented, keeping whatever doubts might still remain in his mind discreetly to himself and perhaps dissipating them entirely by a glance at Miss Bruce who was still standing at the window looking out at the prospect.

How these trivial incidents and words, the elm trees and

---

* Miss Stein never filled in the lines from the *Iliad* in the manuscript of *Fernhurst*. In her later revision of the passage for *The Making of Americans* she deleted the rest of the line so the exact words she intended cannot be known.

the purple hills beyond and the group of people quietly talking remain fixed in the memory. There is a solemnity about a first meeting with those whose lives deeply affect our own that gives a sacredness to the most trivial phrase.

Shortly after this talk the new professor and his wife took their leave. The Dean and Miss Bruce being left together, Miss Thornton began to talk of Redfern but Miss Bruce gave little attention and for the rest of the evening remained lost in a fog of naive realism.

As for Redfern as he walked home it was with a mind filled with delight and interest in the new acquaintance that this afternoon had brought him. He spent much time in feeling and analysing her quality only hoping that she would prove as wonderful as she seemed and desirous to know all that could be known about her, and this little history which he soon learned from college gossip we will now give briefly.

IT HAS BEEN said that the college of Fernhurst in the state of New Jersey was founded by Miss Wyckoff a rich spinster of Virginia under the influence of Miss Thornton the present Dean. Helen Thornton was a member of a family of prominent Quakers in the town of Princeton Pennsylvania, a family which was proud of having bred in three successive generations three remarkable women.

The first of these three was not known beyond her own community of Quakers among whom she had great influence by reason of her strength of will, her powerful intellect, her strong common sense and her deep religious feeling. She kept strictly within the then womanly bounds and carried to its utmost the then practical woman's life with its keen wordly sense, its fervor of emotion and prayer and its devout practical morality.

The daughter of this vigorous woman was known to a wider circle for she went outside of Quaker bounds and sought for truth in all varieties of ecstatic experience. She inherited the quaker temper and mingled with her genuine mystic exaltation a hard common sense and though spending the greater part of her life in examining and actively taking part in all the exaggerated religious enthusiasms of her time she never lost her sense of criticism and judgment and though convinced again and again of the folly and hypocrisy of successive saints never doubted the validity of mystic religious experience.

In the third generation this woman found expression in still wider expreience. Helen Thornton the niece of the famous Quaker mystic abandoned the Quaker doctrines, ceased to expect regeneration from religious experience, found her exaltation in Swinburne and Walter Pater and with pamphlets and a college worked for the rights of women. Miss Thornton was bred in the household of her aunt the Quaker mystic where even before the day of the public preaching of equality for women with men, the doctrine of the superiority of women had been highly developed for in this household a little grand-nephew twelve years of age found it necessary to stand firmly for his rights, "they think so little of men here" he explained.

Bred in this household the conviction in Helen Thornton of the value to the world of women's labor in all fields of work was early acquired and the time being ripe and the ranks of women prepared for battle Miss Thornton became a leader in the movement and did good service for the cause. She learned, preached and struggled for many years, colleges were arising in the land and the time came when she saw that the work so far as it lay with her generation was complete and that the future of the race was in the hands of those who trained the generation that followed after.

For some years she looked in vain for a place to do this work but the chance came at last. Miss Wyckoff was rich elderly and impressed and so now the future of the race to the extent of five hundred young women every four years was in Helen Thornton's hands.

It is hard to desire absolute power, to cherish the ideals of liberty and honor for one's fellows and to be in a position of authority. It was in this situation that the Dean of Fernhurst found herself after her dream of establishing a college for women was realised. It was impossible for her to be in relation with anything or anyone without controlling to the minutest detail and yet this college was to be as a man's, perfect liberty within broad limits, integrity and honor were to prevail.

A system of self government as it was called was inaugurated, the young women themselves were to be the judges of all matters relating to conduct—an admirable plan surely to develop independence and the habit of responsible power but a plan equally adapted to become an effective instrument in the hands of a vigorous, insistent and unmoral nature.

It may seem strange to call unmoral a woman in whom we recognise a pure enthusiasm and a noble devotion for the betterment of her kind, but the Quaker spirit that in one generation could combine shrewd worldly interest with devout devotion and in the next could preserve a hard headed criticism in the midst of a mystic's ecstasy in this last descendant combined a genuine belief in liberty and honor and a disinterested devotion for the uplifting of the

race with an instinct for domination and a persistent indifference to any consideration but expediency in the actual
task of working out her ideal. Few natures were more capable of generous devotion to a whole cause and indeed had
she understood the meaning of her government few natures
would have been more capable of the supreme sacrifice of
renouncing power, but the realisation of such meaning could
never come to her—the methods and details of dominant
superintendence in all its unmoral conditions flowed so
naturally from her position and her instant realisation of the
means adapted to a specific end that the quality of her conduct as an influence could never come to her.

She took only a small share in the actual instruction of
the students for she was no scholar and though a woman of
vigorous mind was not possessed of genuine intellectual
quality. The mystic side of her nature expressed itself in her
delight in Swinburne and Walter Pater and her students
often said that her readings from these men were a rare and
wonderful thing to experience. All the inherited ecstasy was
then expressed and it was in these occasional readings that
she strengthened her influence over her impressionable
young hearers.

Through her influence with Miss Wyckoff she was enabled to keep the college in a flourishing state and to keep
the control of all things from the appointment of instructors
to the furnishing of the dormitory kitchens entirely in her
own hands but she was anxious that in the teaching staff
there should be some one who would be permanent—who
would have great parts and a scholarly mind and would have
no influence to trouble hers and before many years she found
Miss Bruce who ideally fulfilled these demands.

Miss Bruce was a graduate of a Western college and had made some reputation by an article on the philosophy of English poetry. She was appointed by Miss Thornton as assistant in the English department and in a short time had become its head. She was utterly unattached, being an only child whose parents died just before she entered college and was equally detached by her nature from all affairs of the world and was always quite content to remain where she was so long as some [one] took from her all management of practical affairs and left her in peace with her work and her dreams. She was possessed of a sort of transfigured innocence which made a deep impression on the vigorous practical mind of Miss Thornton who while keeping her completely under her control where indeed she liked to keep most people and things that came near her was nevertheless in awe of her blindness to worldly things and of the intellectual power of her clear sensitive mind.

Though Miss Bruce was detached by the quality of her nature from worldly affairs it was not because she loved best dreams and abstract thought, for her deepest interest was in the varieties of human experience and her constant desire was to partake of all human relations but by some quality of her nature she never succeeded in really touching any human creature she knew. Her transfigured innocence too was not an ignorance of the facts of life nor a puritan's instinct indeed her desire was to experience the extreme forms of sensuous life and to make even immoral experience her own. Her detachment was due to an abstracted spirit that could not do what it would and which was evident in her reserved body her shy eyes and gentle face. A passionate desire for worldly experience filled her entirely and she was still waiting for the hand that could tear down the walls that enclosed her and let her escape into a world of humans.

She had been an intelligent comrade to the succession of brilliant young fellows who had one after another filled the philosophical chair at Fernhurst but her interest had remained entirely outside of herself, but in Redfern she felt a new influence. It was more than naive realism that she had caught [a] glimpse of in their first meeting.

In a sense Miss Bruce was quite as unmoral as the Dean herself. Miss Bruce's unmoral quality consisted in her lack of recognition of expediency, her utter indifference to worldly matters. She could lose herself in a relation without any consciousness that other lives and natures were at work and a recognition of such responsibility would come to her no more than to Miss Thornton. It was interesting to observe these women of such different natures ending in the same unmoral temper. The one practical worldly with noble aspirations, a mystic's ecstasy and the power of always adapting the means to a specific end and the other with a mind of a philosopher, a spirit exquisitely sensitive to beauty and a dreamy detached nature with an aspiration for the common lot and a strange incapacity to touch the lives of others.

PHILIP REDFERN WHO was now come to trouble the peace of Fernhurst College was born in a small city in the South western part of the United States. He was the son of a curiously ill assorted pair of parents and his earliest intellectual concept was the realisation of the quality of these two decisive and unharmonised elements in his child life. He remembered too very well his first definite realisation of the quality of women when the inherent contradictions in the claims made by that sex awoke in him much confused thought. He puzzled over the fact that he must give up his chair to and be careful of little girls while at the same time he was taught that the little girl was quite as strong as he and quite as able to use liberty and to perfect action.

His mother was his dear dear friend and from her he received all his definite thoughts and convictions. She was an eager impetuous sensitive creature full of ideal enthusiasms, with moments of clear purpose and vigorous thought but for the most part was prejudiced and inconsequential and apt to accept sensations and impressions as carefully as thought out theories and principles. Her constant rebellion against the pressure of her husband's steady domination found effective expression in the training of her son to be the champion of the rights of women. It would be a sublime proof of poetic justice so she thought for the son of James Redfern to devote his life to the winning of liberty, equality and opportunity for all women.

James Redfern was a man determined always to be master in his own house. He was exaggerated in his courtesy and deference toward all women and never came into personal relations with any human being. He owed his power to his cold reserve his strong will and the perfect rectitude of his conduct. He did not suspect his wife of any set purpose in regard to her son and was too certain of the dominance of his own will to pay much regard to the emotional influences that Mrs. Redfern brought to bear on young Philip. It could never seem possible to him that a man child born in his house could in the end be anything but a rational creature— and fantastic ideals therefore were not to be dreaded and could only exist as the occupation of emotional women and romantic children. He contented himself with demanding from his son obedience and in his presence self-restraint and for the rest relied on Philip's manhood and inherited quality to make him the man he would have him.

This mixture of influences in young Redfern's life resulted in a strange and incalculable nature. The strong emotional flavor of his mother's nature easily awoke in him an exaggerated interest and value for the purely emotional life. The instinct for knowledge and domination were in him

equally strong and from the beginning he devoted himself
to meditation and analysis of the emotions. The constant
spectacle of an armed neutrality between his parents filled
him with an interest in the nature of marriage and the meaning of women.

Like most youngsters bred up in the society of their elders
and those elders of decided quality he had a knowledge of
life quite out of relation to the reality of its experience and
while knowing and accepting many facts that his elders
would have listened to in shocked horror he was really
ignorant of the meaning of the simplest forms of human
relations living as he did in a world all his own where there
was much knowledge, wonderful dreams, keen analysis and
little experience.

From his father he learned scrupulous courtesy and power
of reserve without the fixed standards that governed the
elder Redfern. Philip learned his principles from his mother
and these were of the nature of longings and aspirations
rather than of settled purpose.

When Philip was 21 years old he went to college. He had
never been to a school, his learning had been gathered
largely by himself. Now for the first time he with his brilliant personality, keen intellect, ardent desires, moral aspirations and uncertain principles was to be thrown into familiar
relations with men and women of his own age.

The college of which Redfern became a member was the
typical co-educational college of the Middle West, a completely democratic institution where no one was conscious of
a grandfather and not held responsible for a father, where
inheritance was disregarded and the son of a day laborer if
he was an able fellow had quite as good a chance of leading

his class as the representative of a first family of Virginia or the descendant of a Boston Cabot. This Democracy was too simple and genuine to be discussed and no one was interested whether a man came by his money through generations of gentlemen or whether he earned it in the summer by working on a farm or in the intervals of his college work by acting as janitor to a school building. This Democracy was complete and included simple comradeship between the sexes. The men were simple, direct and earnest in their relations with the girls in the school, treating them with the generosity and kindliness characteristic of the Western man but never doubting for a moment their right to any learning or occupation they were able to acquire.

It was a simple world, uncultured but not crude. The students were earnest experienced men and women who had already struggled solidly with poverty and education. The trend of their minds was toward the natural sciences but in this vigorous open air community there was a true feeling for beauty which showed itself in much out of door wandering for the pure delight in beauty and was beginning to realise itself here and there in healthy sober-minded pictures and sculpture.

It was of this sober-minded earnest moral democratic community that the sophisticated and inexperienced Southerner was now become a part. His moral aspirations found full satisfaction in the serious life of the place and his emotional interest found a new and delightful exercise in the problem of woman that presented itself so strangely here. At his age the return to nature was complete delight for elaboration was not so necessary but that vigor and force made him forgetful of subtlety and refinement. The free,

simple comradeship of the men and women at first filled
him with astonishment and then with delight. He could not
feel himself a part of it, he could not lose the sense of danger
in the presence and companionship of women, his instincts bade him be on guard but his ideal he felt to be here
realised.

Among the many vigorous young women in the place one
Nancy Talbot was conspicuous. She was a blonde good-
looking young woman full of moral purpose and educational
desires. She had an eager earnest intelligence, fixed principles and restless energy. She was the ablest woman student
of her class and she and Redfern soon singled themselves
out from the crowd and in the Western manner had many
long talks in the alcoves of the library and soon developed
the custom of long country walks together.

It was all new, strange and dangerous for the Southern
man and all perfectly simple and matter of course for the
Western girl. They had long talks on the meanings of
things, he discoursing of his life and aims she listening
morally, intensely—understanding sympathising and throwing the protection of her crude new world innocence about
his elaborate old-world meanings.

Their intercourse steadily grew more constant and familiar. Redfern's instincts were dangerous and decadent, his
ideals simple and pure, slowly he realised in this constant
companion the existence of instincts as simple and pure as
his ideals—recognized and did not seek beyond—never asking if the nature was as simple as the feeling or the vision
exalted enough to transcend and so enforce the instinct.

They were tramping through the country one winter's
day plunging vigorously through the snow intoxicated with

cold air and rapid movement and filled with delight in their youth and freedom.

"You are a comrade and a woman" he cried out in his joy. "It is the new world." "Surely" she answered "there is no difference our being together only it is pleasanter and we go faster." "I know it" said Redfern "it is the new world."

This comradeship continued through the year. They spent much time in explaining to each other what neither ever quite understood. He never quite felt the reality of the simple and moral instincts, she never quite realised what it was he did not understand.

One spring day a young boy friend came to see her and all three went out into the country. It was a soft warm day the ground was warm with young life and wet with spring rains. They found a dry hill side and sat down too indolent to wander further. The young friend a boy of seventeen threw himself on the ground with careless freedom and rested his head on Miss Talbot's lap. Redfern could not conceal a start of surprise Miss Talbot smiled and laid her hand caressingly on the boy's head.

The next day Redfern frankly came to her with his perplexity. "I don't understand" he said "was it alright for Johnson to do so yesterday. I almost believed it was my duty to knock him off." "Yes I saw you were surprised" she said and she flushed and looked uneasy. Then resolutely taking her courage in her hands she tried to make him see. "Do you know that to me a Western woman it seems very strange that any one should see any wrong in his action. I have known Johnson all my life and trust his purity as I would my own." Her courage rose with her theme. "Yes I will say it. I have never understood before why you always seemed on guard. Don't you know that so much care on your part is really an insult to a woman's honor. I am a Western woman and believe in men's honesty and in my own, while you—you seem always to doubt both."

She ended steadily, he flushed and looked uneasy. It was a palpable hit, he was pierced in a vital part. He looked at her earnestly, whatever crudity was there, certainly he could not doubt her honesty. It was not a trap, it could not be a new form of deliberate enticement, even though it made a new danger. They walked on, his ideals conquered his instincts, and his devotion was complete. "You wonderful Western woman" he cried out, "Surely you have made a new world."

After two years of marriage Redfern's disillusionment was complete. Miss Talbot was all that she had promised all that he had thought her but that all proved sufficiently inadequate to his needs. She was moral strenuous and pure and sought earnestly after higher things in life and art but her mind was narrow and insistent, her intelligence quick but without grace and harsh and Redfern loved a gentle intelligence. Redfern at best was a hard man to hold, he had no tender fibre to make him gentle to discordant suffering, and when once he was certain that the woman had no message for him there was no appeal. Her narrow eager mind was helpless under the power of his unfailing scrupulous courtesy. He did not use it as a weapon, it was part of him this elaborate chivalry and she though harsh and crude should never cease to receive from him this respect. He knew she must suffer but what could he do. They were man and wife, their minds and natures were separated by great gulfs, it must be again an armed neutrality but this time it was not as with his parents an armed neutrality between equals but with an inferior who could not learn the rules of the game. It was just so much the more unhappy.

Mrs. Redfern never understood what had happened to her. In a dazed blind way she tried all ways of breaking through the walls that confined her. She threw herself against them with impatient energy and again she tried to destroy them piece by piece. She was always thrown back bruised and dazed never quite certain whence came the blow, how it was dealt or why. It was a long agony, she never became wiser or more indifferent, she struggled on always in the same dazed eager way.

Such was the relation between this man and wife when Redfern now twenty nine years of age and having made for himself some reputation in philosophy was called to Fernhurst College to fill the chair of Philosophy there.

IT HAPPENS OFTEN in the twenty-ninth year of a life that all
the forces that have been engaged through the years of
childhood, adolescence and youth in confused and ferocious
combat range themselves in ordered ranks—one is uncertain
of one's aims, meaning and power during these years of
tumultuous growth when aspiration has no relation to fulfillment and one plunges here and there with energy and
misdirection during the storm and stress of the making of
a personality until at last we reach the twenty-ninth year the
straight and narrow gate-way of maturity and life which
was all uproar and confusion narrows down to form and
purpose and we exchange a great dim possibility for a small
hard reality.

Also in our American life where there is no coercion in
custom and it is our right to change our vocation so often
as we have desire and opportunity, it is a common experience
that our youth extends through the whole first twenty-nine

years of our life and it is not till we reach thirty that we find at last that vocation for which we feel ourselves fit and to which we willingly devote continued labor. One smiles as one thinks back over one's varied career—first it was scholarship, then law, then medicine then business then an attempt at art or literature, all begun with enthusiasm pursued a little while with industry, found wanting in meaning and value, abandoned with joy and the next profession ardently adopted and pursued only to be dropped in its turn when found unsuited to the vital need of one's true self. And it must be owned that while much labor is lost to the world in these efforts to secure one's true vocation, nevertheless it makes more completeness in individual life and perhaps in the end will prove as useful to the world—and if we believe that there is more meaning in the choice of love than plain propinquity so we may well believe that there is more meaning in vocation than that it is the thing we first can learn about and win an income with.

Redfern had now come to this fateful twenty-ninth year. He had been a public preacher for women's rights he had been a mathematician, a psychologist and a philosopher, he had married and earned a living  and yet the world was to him without worth or meaning and he longed for a more vital human life than to be an instructor of youth—his theme was humanity, his desire was to be in the great world and of it, he wished for active life among his equals not to pass his days as a guide to the immature and he preferred the criticism of life in fiction to the analysis of the mind in philosophy—and now the time was come in this his twenty-ninth year for the decisive influence in his career.

The instinct which led Philip Redfern to realise the

wondrous quality of gentleness and intelligence in the character of Janet Bruce became soon a deep reverence and
complete devotion which entirely filled his heart and mind
which had before sought in vain for the realisation in this
world of his cherished ideal. Gentleness and intelligence it
was to him the whole expression of the best that life could
give. There seemed so Redfern thought in every look and
gesture of this shy creature, a gentle intelligence and noble
understanding—in motion and repose she seemed wondrous
alike—the tone of her voice were her words ever so awkward
or trivial seemed always to him filled with the same fine
meaning. It was not love that Redfern felt for this shy reserved woman, it was admiration and wonder at the form
in which he had found his ideal. To study her, to understand
her, to analyse her quality and awaken in her a realisation
of her own fine meaning became the business of his life.
Meanwhile as often happens she was unconscious of his
interpretations and was only concerned with questions of
philosophy and the light that Redfern in his keen way threw
on abstruse problems.

Janet Bruce had on her side too her ideals which in this
world she had not found complete. She too longed for the
real world while wrapped away from it by the perverse reserve of her mind and the awkward shyness of her body.
Such friendship as she had yet realised she felt for the Dean
Miss Thornton but it was not a nearness of affection, it was
a recognition of the power of doing and working, and a
deference to the representative of effective action and the
habitual dependence of years of protection. Whatever Miss
Thornton advised or undertook seemed always to Miss
Bruce the best that could be done or effected. She sustained

her end of the relation in being a learned mind, a brilliant teacher and a docile subject. She pursued her way expounding philosophy, imbibing beauty desiring life, never questioning the thing nearest her the dean's methods and morals and her own, interested only in abstract ideas and concrete desire. Her interest in her students was not personal, they were for her mere hearers who were there when she spoke. Shy and awkward as she was, the fact of an audience when her mind was engaged in thought never abashed her, they had no real connection with her world, it was only when forced to regard people as near her and demanding attention that her shyness showed itself in embarrassment. All her life was arranged to leave her untouched and unattached. She liked a social mingling where she took no active part and this in the household of the Dean she had easily. Not regarding worldly things she left all matters that concerned her in the Dean's hands and in active life did always as she was told.

The Dean never suspected in this shy, abstracted, learned creature a desire for sordid life and the common lot. It was not that she did not see the passionate life in this reserved nature but she who knew in herself how abstracted ecstasy could be never once thought that this passionate life could desire a concrete form. She watched her and delighted in her—appreciating her quality as an object and satisfied with her usefulness as a subject. No one could be more wonderful, more useful and more harmless than Janet Bruce.

It was interesting to see what every one but the Dean did see the slow growth of interest to admiration and to love in this awkward reserved woman, unconscious of her meanings and oblivious of the world's eyes, and who made no attempt to disguise or conceal the strength of her feeling. Many students long remembered her as she then appeared slowly sinking from the clouds to the earth under the influence of the brilliant Redfern, her eyes following him first with interest, then admiration, then love, her body slowly filling with yearning and desire, her shy awkward manner making apparent to all what she never thought to conceal.

What Redfern's feeling was these young observers could not see. His feeling was not so simple nor his display of it so open. It was not love that he felt for this shy creature nor had he any illusion about comradeship and platonic affection. His life experience had been to learn that where there was woman there was danger not only through his own affections but by the demand that this sex made upon him. By his extreme chivalry he was always bound to more than fulfill the expectations he gave rise to in the mind of his companions. All this experience had not taught him to keep away from danger, this burned child only learned to dread the fire he could not learn to keep his fingers from it. Indeed this man loved the problem of woman so much that he willingly endured all pain to seek and find the ideal that filled him with such deep unrest and he never tired of meeting and knowing and devoting himself to any woman who promised to fulfill for him his desire and here in Janet Bruce he had found a spirit so delicate so free so gentle and intelligent that no severity of suffering could deter him from seeking the exquisite knowledge that this companionship could give him. He knew that there was danger to her too but felt and not unjustly that she too would willingly pay high for the fresh vision that he brought her. This common danger and common daring to endure it for the hope of deeper knowledge bound these two creatures not tenderly together. The happiest period of all their life was this. This worn ardent man and this worn ardent woman talked, thought, felt and deepened together. They never looked forward content with the deepening knowledge of life and love and sex that each day brought them and Redfern felt in his chivalrous way that all desire that he roused in her mind it was his duty to fulfill and that no price could be too great to pay for the knowledge of her wondrous nature that she so freely gave him and to the last hour of his life he paid this debt for though in after years he yielded many times with many women to his desire to seek and know he never forgot her rights and was ready always at any cost to give her all she wished. Such a gradual growth of feeling is so gentle that many months may be chronicled in a few words but no one's secret life concerns himself alone and this quiet progress was soon to be disturbed.

It was impossible for Redfern to be as unconscious as Miss Bruce of the danger of observation and criticism by the many people by whom they were surrounded. It was true that like many keen observers he was apt to credit others with more blindness than they possessed and to believe that what he saw must by virtue of his greater power of sight be hidden from lesser eyes and minds but even with this strong delusion he could not be entirely blind to the significant smiles and glances that were cast upon them by the young women their obedient students. Before the fact of other's understanding becomes completely felt there are always unconscious pricks and blows that prepare the skin for extra sensitiveness when the burning glass is at length applied. While no one yet has said they see we are dimly aware of uneasiness and fear. Before this relation had reached its height one of that ardent pair was conscious that an end must come and was uneasy and on the look-out for the seeing eye that was to read the story that they lived.

It was easy for the crowd of young women to see what was hidden from the experienced worldly eyes of the dean, who was too blinded by her strength and preconceptions to notice the variation in the manner of this pair who were continually with her. It is not in the old and experienced that danger to secret and subtle relations lies, it is always harsh and crude young things who tear down the sacred veil and with bold eyes pry into the delicate souls and subtle meanings of their elders and translating them into their bald straight words laugh and dissect the things their elders dare not see. While this pair filled with desire and love of life were teaching each other new meanings day by day and the dean always with them her mind engaged with her many duties saw nothing of all this ardent life the whole story had become the gossip of the college. As more violence is always to be dreaded by a crowd of young loafers idle and reckless urging each other on than from a band of hard criminal men so a harsher more relentless interpretation is to be found in the minds of young college women than from most heartless society scandal mongers who in their life have feared and struggled and have the fear of their own condemnation always before their eyes. Then too youth has so little of importance to absorb it and the spectacle of suffering and complexity is still a stimulant and a joy and so this crowd of young women were ready to go farther in meaning to speak straighter in words and to see more clearly the intention than their unscrupulous worldly dean and from them came the words that brought this quiet relation to a disturbed end.

Very likely it would not have been long before Miss Thornton would of herself have noted the disturbed mind and roused feeling of her housemate and constant companion for it must be confessed never did human being make less effort to disguise her feelings and conceal her desires than this shy creature Janet Bruce. She was living in a world of realised dreams and was as little conscious as before of any other life and judgment and thought only of their own two selves and the message they each day brought each other and it required no new effort of attention on Miss Thornton's part when once the suggestion was made to her to realise the whole story as it went and to know the rise and progress of this feeling in her friend whose heart had always lain so open that every one might read it as they passed.

It was in the early fall a year after Redfern's entrance into Fernhurst that Miss Thornton's eyes were opened. It happened in this way one late afternoon she was standing by an open window her eyes fixed on those same distant hills purple in the sunset that the group had watched the day when Redfern first met Janet Bruce. Two students stopped under the window talking and laughing. "Look at Miss Bruce, Helen" one of them cried out "there don't you see her walking into that lilac bush which of course she did not see. Poor thing, she grows more absent-minded every day." "Absent-minded yes her mind is absent enough but her heart is most improperly present, there look at her now, could you possibly guess who it is she sees coming." "I wonder could it be Redfern?" "The girl guessed right the very first time the very first time, the very first time," sang

Helen gayly clapping her friend on the shoulder, "there isn't it a pretty story, look at her and at him." They passed on laughing loudly. Miss Thornton waited until they were out of sight and then stepped into the garden to look too at her and at him. The pair were talking earnestly he as always courteous, inscrutable, suggestive, she her whole ardent soul in her eyes her body strained with new desire, her gentle face filled with delight. Miss Thornton gave a long look and then withdrew into the house to think it out alone.

IT IS THE FRENCH habit to consider that in the usual grouping
of two and an extra which humanity so constantly supplies it
is the two that get something from it all who are of importance and whose claim should be considered—the American
mind accustomed to waste happiness and be reckless of joy
finds morality more important than ecstasy and the lonely
extra of more value than the happy two. To our new world
feeling the sadness of pain has more dignity than the beauty
of joy. It takes time to learn the value of happiness, and in
our hasty sandwich variety of intercourse that knowledge is
never acquired. Truly a single moment snatched out of a
distracted existence is hardly worth the trouble it is to seize
it and to obtain such it is wasteful to inflict pain—it is only
the cultivators of an infinite leisure who have time to feel
the gentle approach, the slow rise, the deep ecstasy and the
full flow of joy and for these pain is of little value, a thing

not to be remembered, and it is only the loss of joy that counts.

Poor Nancy Redfern eager, anxious and moral had little understanding of the sanctity of joy and a very keen realisation of the misery of pain. She understood as little now as before what all this was that had come upon her and she still tried to arrange and explain it by her straight Western morality and her narrow new world humanity. She could not escape the knowledge that something stronger than community of interest bound her husband and Miss Bruce together. She tried resolutely to interpret it all in Western terms of comradeship and greater intellectual equality never admitting for a moment the conception of a possible marital disloyalty a conception so foreign to the moral American mind. It was as easy for her to think a man of her people a thief or a prisoner as to conceive him false to his plain duty—these were things that were simply not done in coeducational middle western America. But in spite of these standards and convictions she was filled with a vague uneasiness that had a different meaning than the habitual struggle against the hard wall of chivalrous courtesy that Redfern had erected before her.

This struggle in her mind showed itself clearly when she was in the company of her husband and Miss Bruce and many students noticed and remembered for years the painful picture that she made in those afternoons when the faculty, the wives and a group of students met together for the social life of the college. She would sit conscientiously bending her mind to the self-imposed task of understanding and development—when in the immediate circle of talkers that included her husband and Miss Bruce she gave anxious and impartial attention to the words of one and the other occasionally joining in the talk by an anxious inquiry and receiving always from Redfern the courteous deference that he extended to all women. She resolutely repressed any movement of suspicion or irritation and listened with admiring attention particularly to Miss Bruce who genuinely unconscious of all this stifled misery paid her in return scant attention. When she was not in the immediate group of talkers with these two, with the same moral zeal she kept her attention on the person with whom she was talking and succeeded to a marvel in controlling the instinct for furtive glances in their direction and showed the burden of her feeling only in the anxious care with which she listened and talked, the restless under-current in her blonde good-looking face and the straining clasp of her two hands as they lay in her lap.

She was not to be left much longer to work out her own conclusions. One afternoon in the late fall in the second year of their life at Fernhurst, Mrs. Redfern had good reason to remember it, the dean Miss Thornton came to the room where she was sitting alone studying a Greek grammar and putting aside all barriers of courtesy and gentleness the dean in her abrupt way spoke directly of the object of her visit. "Mrs. Redfern", she began "you probably know something of the gossip that is at present going on among the students. I want you to keep Mr. Redfern in order, I cannot allow him to make Miss Bruce the subject of scandalous talk. The instructors in a woman's college cannot be too careful of their actions." She stopped and looked steadily at the anxious uneasy woman who was dazed by this sudden statement of her own suspicion. "I, I don't understand," she stammered. "I think you understand quite well, if not any student in the place can enlighten you. I say nothing against Mr. Redfern, I say only that you must keep him in order or he must leave the college. I depend upon you to speak to him about it" and with this she departed.

This action on Miss Thornton's part showed deep wisdom. She knew very well the small influence that Mrs. Redfern had over her husband and she took this method of attack only because it was the only one open to her. Her instinct for human quality told her that even she could not get within Redfern's polished guard. Janet Bruce she knew would turn toward her an abstracted mind, an unseeing eye and unhearing ear. Mrs. Redfern too could accomplish nothing by direct action but she was a woman and jealous and there was little doubt, so the dean thought, that before long she would effect some change. The Dean could not cause Redfern to leave in the midst of a term without danger of involving Miss Bruce in a serious scandal. It was a difficult point to settle and Miss Thornton with her instinct for the straight act to a desired end chose this of putting Redfern's wife on guard. Her suspicion might force Redfern to circumspection and if the dean could save Miss Bruce from the odium of open scandal all might yet be well and Fernhurst when this restless man would leave it as leave he must at the end of the year, would settle down to peace again. Even if Miss Bruce's desires should continue, the scandal would keep itself outside of college grounds and the Dean with her firm hand would keep Miss Bruce from public blame. Miss Thornton had thought it out very well alone.

Nancy Redfern's mind was now a confusion worse con-founded. Miss Thornton had added nothing to her facts nor had she accused Redfern of anything but indiscretion but nevertheless her statement had made a certainty of what Mrs. Redfern had regarded as an impossibility. She had no new evidence of Redfern's marital disloyalty but there was now no corner of her mind that was not convinced of his iniquity. She sat there long and long thinking over again and again the same weary round of thoughts and terrors. She knew she was powerless to change him, she could only try to get the evidence to condemn him. Did she want it, if she had it she must act on it, she dreaded to obtain it and could no longer exist without it. She knew she was power-less to get within Redfern's polished guard. She must watch him and find it all out without questioning, must learn it by seeing and hearing and she felt dimly a terror of the things she might be caught doing to obtain it—she dreaded the condemnation of Redfern's chivalrous honor. She did not doubt his disloyalty she was convinced of that in her inmost soul and she still feared to lose his respect for her sense of honor. "He is dishonorable, all his action is deceit," she said to herself again and again but she found no comfort in this thought, she knew there was a difference and she respected his standard more than her own justification.

In the long weary days that followed she was torn by these desires, she must watch him always and secretly, she must gain the knowledge she dreaded to possess, and she must be deeply ashamed of the means she must pursue. Mrs. Red-fern's manner of which you may be sure the student crowd were intensely observant became in these days much

changed. She was no longer able to listen to others when
her husband and Miss Bruce were in her presence, she dared
not keep an open watch but her observation was unceasing
and did not escape the keen observers who with eager interest were watching this drama work itself out in their midst.

Redfern was not wholly unconscious of this change in his
wife's manner perhaps more in the relief that she ceased her
eager efforts to please him than in the annoyance of her
suspicious watching. Redfern was a man too much on guard
to fear surprise and with all his experience too ignorant of
women's ways to see danger where danger really lay. Eagerly
did the student crowd watch and discuss the varying
changes in the manners of this interesting quartet so constantly before them. The difficulty of private time for Redfern and Miss Bruce steadily increased, the students
watched openly, joyously, tauntingly, Mrs. Redfern watched
secretly, furtively, incessantly, the dean watched abruptly,
annoyingly, intermittently, there was no moment when they
were without an audience and that audience keen in observation and ready from one motive or another to interpret
largely slight variations in tone and manner.

Redfern moved in the midst of this maze of watching
womanhood half conscious, half unconscious. He was aware
how much they were observed, but he thought slightly of
the quality of that observing. The danger and the mystery—
the beauty of the movement of Janet Bruce, self-absorbed,
intense, free, with her tall reserved body gentle face and
shy eyes through this mass of staring creatures, so he called
them in his mind, stirred his blood with keen delight. He
had no fear, there would be no open war, he knew all must

be shrouded in convention and decent conduct and he knew himself strong to thread such subtle mazes.

Private intercourse was now become impossible within college bounds and public intercourse uncomfortable. These two ardent, difficult creatures had been separated and there had been no open scandal. The dean had managed very well a very difficult matter but the end was not yet. Strange stories began to be told among the students. One lucky creature recited with glee the history of an ecstatic meeting and a tragic parting that she had witnessed in the center of Camden the chief railway station of the neighboring town of Trenton. "Naive realism is most absorbing, they never saw me though I almost fell into them—oh to see her look at him and him at her" she ended joyously and her audience filled with the delight of this picture separated with a burst of noisy laughter.

Another student watched the pair joined in rapt ecstasy in the center of a crowded street-car. She rehearsed the dialogue as she had interpreted it from a distance and became famous for the part throughout the college. "Give us Redfern and the Bruce in the street-car doing naive realism!" became the cry at all the gatherings of students where the hostess had been fortunate in securing the attendance of this lucky clever one.

These histories were all true—these two ardent creatures seized their ecstasy where they could, this shy reserved abstracted woman for whom there was no outer world filled with mockery, and this chivalrous, devoted, deeply attentive man who knew the outside world to disregard it, but the end was not yet though Redfern's college days were numbered. No the end was not yet for Nancy Redfern had not gained the evidence that she so dreaded and was so steadily moved to obtain.

It was the end of May and one late afternoon Mrs. Redfern filled with her sad past and sadder future, sat in her room drearily watching the young leaves shining brilliantly green in the warm sunshine of the long row of elms that stretched away through the village toward the green hills that rose so beautifully beyond. Mrs. Redfern knew very well the feel of that earth warm with young life and wet with spring rains, knew it as part of her dreary life that seemed to have lasted always. As she sat there in sadness, for one little while that unquiet creature was still, the restless eagerness in her blonde good-looking face was gone and her hands lay clasped quietly without straining—she had yielded her spirit to the languor of that mournful springtime and sadness had become stronger in her than desire. She sat there in quiet sadness for some minutes and then the old eager anxiety sprang into full life, her hands strained in their clasp the anxious unrest filled her blonde face and troubled her weary eyes and she attempted to fix an earnest attention on the book on the reading desk at her side. Redfern came into the house and passed into his own study. He remained there a short while and then was called away by a message from the Dean. As soon as he was out of sight Mrs. Redfern arose and went into his room. She walked up to his desk and opening his portfolio saw a letter in his writing. She scarcely hesitated so eager was she to read it. She read it to the end—she had her evidence. She turned with the letter still in her hand and faced Redfern who had come back. Their eyes met, Redfern was sinful, she was dishonorable, her eyes fell and she was ashamed. "I found it by accident" she stammered in confusion, "I did not know it was private." Redfern received the paper in silence and she hurried from the room. "That was a brutally discourteous act" Redfern said to himself some hours later, "I should have accepted her apology, of course she lied but I ought not to have shown that I thought so. . . "

THIS WAS THE END of Redfern's teaching experience—for the rest of his days he lived the difficult life of a man of letters who aspires to be an effective agent in the actual working of a boisterous world. Such lives are hard in the living and for the most part poor in result. He plunged deeply into the political life of his time and failed everywhere. In this life as in all his human relations his instincts gave the lie to his ideals and his ideals to his instincts. In one of his rare moments of honest self-estimate he admitted this. "Lathrop tells a lie as if it were the truth" he said speaking of another man of letters "and I tell the truth as if it were a lie." It was painful to witness the life of this man, to see him go up again and again against the evil spirit in him, go up with unwearied courage only to meet with certain defeat. He was himself the only one of all the lookers on who dreamed of victory. The others whether watching with indifference, with deep sympathy or stern condemnation with malicious or righteous triumph knew that he would fail, but he always struggled on filled to the very end with hope and courage, always defeated and always ready to make the fresh assault.

"A sad example of a literary man without character" said one of his old colleagues but that was not the whole truth, he had character, yes and high ideals and courage, too, for the fight but his instincts always thrust him into danger and his chivalry bound him to a losing fight. He did not know how to win, how to avoid battle or how to yield—he only learned to dread the fire, he never learned to keep his fingers from it—the elements were so mixed in him that his best was no help against his worst and his worst never won the victory over his best—he remained always a hopeless inextricable mess.

"A wonderful man! to produce in two years' time an admirable piece of metaphysical writing, a clever novel and a political biography—what a brilliant mind it is, and with it all he cannot earn a living or a decent recognition from his fellows" said of him an old professor who had been a sympathetic witness of his disturbed career. "What is the use of his cleverness when he treated Nancy Redfern so badly" said the professor's wife indignantly "of course he wouldn't succeed, the hypocrite, and there is the poor creature living alone in Germany, studying Greek so that she may become worthy of his companionship! I have no patience with him." "But his work is so good, so brilliant" said the professor. "Well it ought not to be and you haven't any business to say it is, poor Nancy Redfern" answered his wife. No the elements were so mixed in him that his best was no better than his worst—he never ceased to struggle and he never ceased to fail.

To the last hour of his life he was true to his ideal of gentleness and intelligence that he had found so wondrously expressed in Janet Bruce. She never compromised herself further in the eyes of the world but strange stories still floated about Fernhurst college. Redfern and Miss Bruce had been seen so it was said coming out of a hotel each with their own dress-suit case—other strange rumors about them were current but the energy and discretion of Miss Thornton kept them from ever becoming more than rumor and gradually they died away. Patiently and quietly the dean worked it out and before many years she had regained all property rights in this shy learned creature. It was sometimes disconcerting when Miss Bruce was moved abruptly to inquire concerning Redfern from people who had known him but this too gradually faded away and Fernhurst was itself again and the two very interesting personalities in the place were the dean Miss Thornton with her friend Miss Bruce in their very same place.

# Q.E.D.

PHEBE: Good shepherd, tell this youth what 'tis to love.

SILVIUS: It is to be all made of sighs and tears;
And so am I for Phebe.

PHEBE: And I for Ganymede.

ORLANDO: And I for Rosalind.

ROSALIND: And I for no woman.

SILVIUS: It is to be all made of faith and service;
And so am I for Phebe.

PHEBE: And I for Ganymede.

ORLANDO: And I for Rosalind.

ROSALIND: And I for no woman.

SILVIUS: It is to be all made of fantasy,
All made of passion, and all made of wishes;
All adoration, duty, and observance,
All humbleness, all patience, and impatience,
All purity, all trial, all deservings;
And so am I for Phebe.

PHEBE: And so am I for Ganymede.

ORLANDO: And so am I for Rosalind.

ROSALIND: And so am I for no woman.

PHEBE: If this be so, why blame you me to love you?

SILVIUS: If this be so, why blame you me to love you?

ORLANDO: If this be so, why blame you me to love you?

ROSALIND: Who do you speak to, 'Why blame you me to love
you?'

ORLANDO: To her that is not here, nor doth not hear.

ROSALIND: Pray you, no more of this: 'tis like the howling of
Irish wolves against the moon.

AS YOU LIKE IT 5:2

# Book 1: ADELE

THE LAST MONTH of Adele's life in Baltimore had been such a succession of wearing experiences that she rather regretted that she was not to have the steamer all to herself. It was very easy to think of the rest of the passengers as mere wooden objects; they were all sure to be of some abjectly familiar type that one knew so well that there would be no need of recognising their existence, but these two people who would be equally familiar if they were equally little known would as the acquaintance progressed, undoubtedly expose large tracts of unexplored and unknown qualities, filled with new and strange excitements. A little knowledge is not a dangerous thing, on the contrary it gives the most cheerful sense of completeness and content.

"Oh yes" Adele said to a friend the morning of her sailing "I would rather be alone just now but I dare say they will be amusing enough. Mabel Neathe of course I know pretty well; that is we haven't any very vital relations but we have drunk much tea together and sentimentalised over it in a fashion more or less interesting. As for Helen Thomas I don't know her at all although we have met a number of times. Her talk is fairly amusing and she tells very good stories, but she isn't my kind much. Still I don't think it will be utterly hopeless. Heigho it's an awful grind; new countries, new people and new experiences all to see, to know and to understand; old countries, old friends and old experiences to keep on seeing, knowing and understanding."

They had been several days on the ship and had learned to make themselves very comfortable. Their favorite situation had some disadvantages; it was directly over the screw and they felt the jar every time that it left the water, but then the weather was not very rough and so that did not happen very frequently.

All three of them were college bred American women of the wealthier class but with that all resemblance between them ended. Their appearance, their attitudes and their talk both as to manner and to matter showed the influence of different localities, different forebears and different family ideals. They were distinctly American but each one at the same time bore definitely the stamp of one of the older civilisations, incomplete and frustrated in this American version but still always insistent.

The upright figure was that of Helen Thomas. She was the American version of the English handsome girl. In her ideal completeness she would have been unaggressively determined, a trifle brutal and entirely impersonal; a woman of passions but not of emotions, capable of long sustained action, incapable of regrets. In this American edition it amounted at its best to no more than a brave bluff. In the strength of her youth Helen still thought of herself as the unfrustrated ideal; she had as yet no suspicion of her weakness, she had never admitted to herself her defeats.

As Mabel Neathe lay on the deck with her head in Helen's lap, her attitude of awkward discomfort and the tension of her long angular body sufficiently betrayed her New England origin. It is one of the peculiarities of American womanhood that the body of a coquette often encloses the soul of a prude and the angular form of a spinster is possessed by a nature of the tropics. Mabel Neathe had the angular body of a spinster but the face told a different story. It was pale yellow brown in complexion and thin in the temples and forehead; heavy about the mouth, not with the weight of flesh but with the drag of unidealised passion, continually sated and continually craving. The long formless chin accentuated the lack of moral significance. If the contour had been a little firmer the face would have been baleful. It was a face that in its ideal completeness would have belonged to the decadent days of Italian greatness. It would never now express completely a nature that could hate subtly and poison deftly. In the American woman the aristocracy had become vulgarised and the power weakened. Having gained nothing moral, weakened by lack of adequate development of its strongest instincts, this nature expressed itself in a face no longer dangerous but only unillumined and unmoral, but yet with enough suggestion of the older aristocratic use to keep it from being merely contemptibly dishonest.

The third member of the group had thrown herself prone on the deck with the freedom of movement and the simple instinct for comfort that suggested a land of laziness and sunshine. She nestled close to the bare boards as if accustomed to make the hard earth soft by loving it. She made just a few wriggling movements to adapt her large curves to the projecting boards of the deck, gave a sigh of satisfaction and murmured "How good it is in the sun."

They all breathed in the comfort of it for a little time and then Adele raising herself on her arm continued the interrupted talk. "Of course I am not logical," she said "logic is all foolishness. The whole duty of man consists in being reasonable and just. I know Mabel that you don't consider that an exact portrait of me but nevertheless it is true. I am reasonable because I know the difference between understanding and not understanding and I am just because I have no opinion about things I don't understand."

"That sounds very well indeed" broke in Helen "but somehow I don't feel that your words really express you. Mabel tells me that you consider yourself a typical middle-class person, that you admire above all things the middle-class ideals and yet you certainly don't seem one in thoughts or opinions. When you show such a degree of inconsistency how can you expect to be believed?"

"The contradiction isn't in me," Adele said sitting up to the occasion and illustrating her argument by vigorous gestures, "it is in your perverted ideas. You have a foolish notion that to be middle-class is to be vulgar, that to cherish the ideals of respectability and decency is to be commonplace and that to be the mother of children is to be low. You tell me that I am not middle-class and that I can believe in none of these things because I am not vulgar, commonplace and low, but it is just there where you make your mistake.

You don't realise the important fact that virtue and vice have it in common that they are vulgar when not passionately given. You think that they carry within them a different power. Yes they do because they have different world-values, but as for their relation to vulgarity, it is as true of vice as of virtue that you can't sell what should be passionately given without forcing yourself into many acts of vulgarity and the chances are that in endeavoring to escape the vulgarity of virtue, you will find yourselves engulfed in the vulgarity of vice. Good gracious! here I am at it again. I never seem to know how to keep still, but you both know already that I have the failing of my tribe. I believe in the sacred rites of conversation even when it is a monologue."

"Oh don't stop yourself," Mabel said quietly, "it is entertaining and we know you don't believe it." "Alright" retorted Adele "you think that I have no principles because I take everything as it comes but that is where you are wrong. I say bend again and again but retain your capacity for regaining an upright position, but you will have to learn it in your own way, I am going to play with the sunshine." And then there was a long silence.

They remained there quietly in the warm sunshine looking at the bluest of blue oceans, with the wind moulding itself on their faces in great soft warm chunks. At last Mabel sat up with a groan. "No," she declared, "I cannot any longer make believe to myself that I am comfortable. I haven't really believed it any of the time and the jar of that screw is unbearable. I am going back to my steamer chair." Thereupon ensued between Helen and Mabel the inevitable and interminable offer and rejection of companionship that politeness demands and the elaborate discussion and explanation that always ensues when neither offer nor rejection are sincere. At last Adele broke in with an impatient "I always did thank God I wasn't born a woman," whereupon Mabel hastily bundled her wraps and disappeared down the companion-way.

The two who were left settled down again quietly but somehow the silence now subtly suggested the significance of their being alone together. This consciousness was so little expected by either of them that each was uncertain of the other's recognition of it. Finally Adele lifted her head and rested it on her elbow. After another interval of silence she began to talk very gently without looking at her companion.

"One hears so much of the immensity of the ocean but that isn't at all the feeling that it gives me," she began. "My quarrel with it is that it is the most confined space in the world. A room just big enough to turn around in is immensely bigger. Being on the ocean is like being placed under a nice clean white inverted saucer. All the boundaries are so clear and hard. There is no escape from the knowledge of the limits of your prison. Doesn't it give you too a sensation of intolerable confinement?" She glanced up at her companion who was looking intently at her but evidently had not been hearing her words. After a minute Helen continued the former conversation as if there had been no interruption. "Tell me" she said "what do you really mean by calling yourself middle-class? From the little that I have seen of you I think that you are quite right when you say that you are reasonable and just but surely to understand others and even to understand oneself is the

last thing a middle-class person cares to do." "I never
claimed to be middle-class in my intellect and in truth" and
Adele smiled brightly. "I probably have the experience of
all apostles, I am rejected by the class whose cause I preach
but that has nothing to do with the case. I simply contend
that the middle-class ideal which demands that people be
affectionate, respectable, honest and content, that they avoid
excitements and cultivate serenity is the ideal that appeals
to me, it is in short the ideal of affectionate family life, of
honorable business methods."

"But that means cutting passion quite out of your scheme
of things!"

"Not simple moral passions, they are distinctly of it, but
really my chief point is a protest against this tendency of so
many of you to go in for things simply for the sake of an
experience. I believe strongly that one should do things
either for the sake of the thing done or because of definite
future power which is the legitimate result of all education.
Experience for the paltry purpose of having had it is to me
both trivial and immoral. As for passion" she added with
increasing earnestness "you see I don't understand much
about that. It has no reality for me except as two varieties,
affectionate comradeship on the one hand and physical
passion in greater or less complexity on the other and against
the cultivation of that latter I have an almost puritanic
horror and that includes an objection to the cultivation of
it in any of its many disguised forms. I have a sort of notion
that to be capable of anything more worth while one must
have the power of idealising another and I don't seem to
have any of that."

After a pause Helen explained it. "That is what makes it

possible for a face as thoughtful and strongly built as yours
to be almost annoyingly unlived and youthful and to be almost foolishly happy and content." There was another
silence and then Adele said with conviction "I could undertake to be an efficient pupil if it were possible to find
an efficient teacher," and then they left it there between
them.

In the long idle days that followed an affectionate relation
gradually grew between these two. In the chilly evenings as
Adele lay at her side on the deck, Helen would protect her
from the wind and would allow her hand to rest gently on
her face and her fingers to flutter vaguely near her lips. At
such times Adele would have dimly a sense of inward resistance, a feeling that if she were not so sluggish she would
try to decide whether she should yield or resist but she felt
too tired to think, to yield or to resist and so she lay there
quite quiet, quite dulled.

These relations formed themselves so gradually and
gently that only the nicest observer could have noted any
change in the relations of the three. Their intercourse was
apparently very much what it had been. There were long
conversations in which Adele vehemently and with much
picturesque vividness explained her views and theories of
manners, people and things, in all of which she was steadily
opposed by Helen who differed fundamentally in all her
convictions, aspirations and illusions.

Mabel would listen always with immense enjoyment as if
it were a play and enacted for her benefit and queerly enough
although the disputants were much in earnest in their talk

and in their oppositions, it was a play and enacted for her benefit.

One afternoon Adele was lying in her steamer chair yielding herself to a sense of physical weariness and to the disillusionment of recent failures. Looking up she saw Helen looking down at her. Adele's expression changed. "I beg your pardon" she said "I didn't know any one was near. Forgive the indecency of my having allowed the dregs of my soul to appear on the surface." "It is I who ought to apologise for having observed you" Helen answered gravely. Adele gave her a long look of unimpassioned observation. "I certainly never expected to find you one of the most gentle and considerate of human kind," she commented quietly and then Helen made it clearer. "I certainly did not expect that you would find me so," she answered.

This unemphasised interchange still left them as before quite untouched. It was an impartial statement from each one, a simple observation on an event. Time passed and still no charged words, glances or movements passed between them, they gave no recognition of each other's consciousness.

One evening lying there in the darkness yielding to a suggestion rather than to an impulse Adele pressed the fluttering fingers to her lips. The act was to herself quite without emphasis and without meaning.

The next night as she lay down in her berth, she suddenly awakened out of her long emotional apathy. For the first time she recognised the existence of Helen's consciousness and realised how completely ignorant she was both as to its extent and its meaning. She meditated a long time. Finally she began to explain to herself. "No I don't understand it at all," she said. "There are so many possibilities and then there is Mabel," and she dropped into another meditation. Finally it took form. "Of course Helen may be just drifting as I was, or else she may be interested in seeing how far I will go before my principles get in my way or whether they will get in my way at all, and then again it's barely possible that she may really care for me and again she may be playing some entirely different game.—And then there is Mabel. —Apparently she is not to know, but is that real; does it make any difference; does Helen really care or is she only doing it secretly for the sense of mystery. Surely she is right. I am very ignorant. Here after ten days of steady companionship I haven't the vaguest conception of her, I haven't the slightest clue to her or her meanings. Surely I must be very stupid" and she shook her head disconsolately "and to-morrow is our last day together and I am not likely to find out then. I would so much like to know" she continued "but I can see no way to it, none at all except," and she smiled to herself "except by asking her and then I have no means of knowing whether she is telling me the truth. Surely all is vanity for I once thought I knew something about women," and with a long sigh of mystification she composed herself to sleep.

The next afternoon leaving Mabel comfortable with a book, Adele, with a mind attuned to experiment wandered back with Helen to their favorite outlook. It was a sparkling day and Adele threw herself on the deck joyous with the sunshine and the blue. She looked up at Helen for a minute and then began to laugh, her eyes bright with amusement. "Now what?" asked Helen. "Oh nothing much, I was just thinking of the general foolishness, Mabel and you and I. Don't you think it's pretty foolish?" There was nothing mocking in her face nothing but simple amusement.

Helen's face gave no response and made no comment but soon she hit directly with words. "I am afraid" she said "that after all you haven't a nature much above passionettes. You are so afraid of losing your moral sense that you are not willing to take it through anything more dangerous than a mud-puddle."

Adele took it frankly, her smile changed to meditation. "Yes there is something in what you say," she returned "but after all if one has a moral sense there is no necessity in being foolhardy with it. I grant you it ought to be good for a swim of a mile or two, but surely it would be certain death to let it loose in mid-ocean. It's not a heroic point of view I admit, but then I never wanted to be a hero, but on the other hand," she added "I am not anxious to cultivate cowardice. I wonder—" and then she paused. Helen gave her a little while and then left her.

Adele continued a long time to look out on the water. "I wonder" she said to herself again. Finally it came more definitely. "Yes I wonder. There isn't much use in wondering about Helen. I know no more now than I did last night and I am not likely to be much wiser. She gives me no means of taking hold and the key of the lock is surely not in me. It can't be that she really cares enough to count, no that's impossible," and she relapsed once more into silence.

Her meditations again took form. "As for me is it another little indulgence of my superficial emotions or is there any possibility of my really learning to realise stronger feelings. If it's the first I will call a halt promptly and at once. If it's the second I won't back out, no not for any amount of moral sense," and she smiled to herself. "Certainly it is very difficult to tell. The probabilities are that this is only another one of the many and so I suppose I had better quit and leave it. It's the last day together and so to be honorable I must quit at once." She then dismissed it all and for some time longer found it very pleasant there playing with the brightness. At last she went forward and joined the others. She sat down by Helen's side and promptly changed her mind. It was really quite different, her moral sense had lost its importance.

Helen was very silent that evening all through the tedious table d'hôte dinner. The burden of the entertainment rested on Adele and she supported it vigorously. After dinner they all went back to their old station. It was a glorious night that last one on the ship. They lay on the deck the stars bright overhead and the wine-colored sea following fast behind the ploughing screw. Helen continued silent, and Adele all through her long discourse on the superior quality of California starlight and the incidents of her childhood with which she was regaling Mabel, all through this talk she still wondered if Helen really cared.

"Was I brutal this afternoon?" she thought it in definite words "and does she really care? If she does it would be only decent of me to give some sign of contrition for if she does care I am most woefully ashamed of my levity, but if she doesn't and is just playing with me then I don't want to apologise." Her mind slowly alternated between these two possibilities. She was beginning to decide in favor of the more generous one, when she felt Helen's hand pressing gently over her eyes. At once the baser interpretation left her mind quite completely. She felt convinced of Helen's rare intensity and generosity of feeling. It was the first recognition of mutual dependence.

Steadily the night grew colder clearer and more beautiful. Finally Mabel left them. They drew closer together and in a little while Adele began to question. "You were very generous," she said "tell me how much do you care for me." "Care for you my dear" Helen answered "more than you know and less than you think." She then began again with some abruptness "Adele you seem to me capable of very genuine friendship. You are at once dispassionate in your judgments and loyal in your feelings; tell me will we be friends?" Adele took it very thoughtfully. "One usually knows very definitely when there is no chance of an acquaintance becoming a friendship but on the other hand it is impossible to tell in a given case whether there is. I really don't know," she said. Helen answered her with fervor. "I honor you for being honest." "Oh honest," returned Adele lightly. "Honesty is a selfish virtue. Yes I am honest enough." After a long pause she began again meditatively, "I wonder if either of us has the slightest idea what is going on in the other's head." "That means that you think me very wicked?" Helen asked. "Oh no" Adele responded

"I really don't know enough about you to know whether you are wicked or not. Forgive me I don't mean to be brutal" she added earnestly "but I really don't know."

There was a long silence and Adele looked observingly at the stars. Suddenly she felt herself intensely kissed on the eyes and on the lips. She felt vaguely that she was apathetically unresponsive. There was another silence. Helen looked steadily down at her. "Well!" she brought out at last. "Oh" began Adele slowly "I was just thinking." "Haven't you ever stopped thinking long enough to feel?" Helen questioned gravely. Adele shook her head in slow negation. "Why I suppose if one can't think at the same time I will never accomplish the feat of feeling. I always think. I don't see how one can stop it. Thinking is a pretty continuous process" she continued "sometimes it's more active than at others but it's always pretty much there." "In that case I had better leave you to your thoughts" Helen decided. "Ah! don't go," exclaimed Adele. "I don't want to stir." "Why not?" demanded Helen. "Well" Adele put it tentatively "I suppose it's simply inertia." "I really must go" repeated Helen gently, there was no abruptness in her voice or movement. Adele sat up, Helen bent down, kissed her warmly and left.

Adele sat for a while in a dazed fashion. At last she shook her head dubiously and murmured, "I wonder if it was inertia." She sat some time longer among the tossed rugs and finally with another dubious head-shake said with mock sadness, "I asked the unavailing stars and they replied not, I am afraid it's too big for me" and then she stopped thinking. She kept quiet some time longer watching the pleasant night. At last she gathered the rugs together and started to go below. Suddenly she stopped and dropped heavily on a bench. "Why" she said in a tone of intense interest, "it's like a bit of mathematics. Suddenly it does itself and you begin to see," and then she laughed. "I am afraid Helen wouldn't think much of that if it's only seeing. However I never even thought I saw before and I really do think I begin to see. Yes it's very strange but surely I do begin to see."

All during the summer Adele did not lose the sense of having seen, but on the other hand her insight did not deepen. She meditated abundantly on this problem and it always ended with a childlike pride in the refrain "I did see a little, I certainly did catch a glimpse."

She thought of it as she and her brother lay in the evenings on the hill-side at Tangiers feeling entirely at home with the Moors who in their white garments were rising up and down in the grass like so many ghostly rabbits. As they lay there agreeing and disagreeing in endless discussion with an intensity of interest that long familiarity had in no way diminished, varied by indulgence in elaborate foolishness and reminiscent jokes, she enjoyed to the full the sense of family friendship. She felt that her glimpse had nothing to do with all this. It belonged to another less pleasant and more incomplete emotional world. It didn't illuminate this one and as yet it was not very alluring in itself but as she remarked to herself at the end of one of her unenlightening discussions on this topic, "It is something one ought to know. It seems almost a duty."

Sitting in the court of the Alhambra watching the swallows
fly in and out of the crevices of the walls, bathing in the soft
air filled with the fragrance of myrtle and oleander and letting the hot sun burn her face and the palms of her hands,
losing herself thus in sensuous delight she would murmur
again and again "No it isn't just this, it's something more,
something different. I haven't really felt it but I have caught
a glimpse."

One day she was sitting on a hill-side looking down at
Granada desolate in the noon-day sun. A young Spanish girl
carrying a heavy bag was climbing up the dry, brown hill.
As she came nearer they smiled at each other and exchanged
greetings. The child sat down beside her. She was one of
those motherly little women found so often in her class, full
of gentle dignity and womanly responsibility.

They sat there side by side with a feeling of complete
companionship, looking at each other with perfect compre-
hension, their intercourse saved from the interchange of
common-places by their ignorance of each other's language.
For some time they sat there, finally they arose and walked
on together. They parted as quiet friends part, and as long
as they remained in sight of each other they turned again
and again and signed a gentle farewell.

After her comrade had disappeared Adele returned to her
insistent thought. "A simple experience like this is very perfect, can my new insight give me realler joys?" she questioned. "I doubt it very much" she said. "It doesn't deepen
such experiences in fact it rather annoyingly gets in my way
and disturbs my happy serenity. Heavens what an egotist I

am!'' she exclaimed and then she devoted herself to the sunshine on the hills.

Later on she was lying on the ground reading again Dante's *Vita Nuova*. She lost herself completely in the tale of Dante and Beatrice. She read it with absorbed interest for it seemed now divinely illuminated. She rejoiced abundantly in her new understanding and exclaimed triumphantly "At last I begin to see what Dante is talking about and so there is something in my glimpse and it's alright and worth while" and she felt within herself a great content.

# Book 2: *MABEL NEATHE*

## 1

MABEL NEATHE'S ROOM fully met the habit of many hours of unaggressive lounging. She had command of an exceptional talent for atmosphere. The room with its very good shape, dark walls but mediocre furnishings and decorations was more than successfully unobtrusive, it had perfect quality. It had always just the amount of light necessary to make mutual observation pleasant and yet to leave the decorations in obscurity or rather to inspire a faith in their being good.

It is true of rooms as of human beings that they are bound to have one good feature and as a Frenchwoman dresses to that feature in such fashion that the observer must see that and notice nothing else, so Mabel Neathe had arranged her room so that one enjoyed one's companions and observed consciously only the pleasant fire-place.

But the important element in the success of the room as atmosphere consisted in Mabel's personality. The average guest expressed it in the simple comment that she was a perfect hostess, but the more sympathetic observers put it that it was not that she had the manners of a perfect hostess but the more unobtrusive good manners of a gentleman.

The chosen and they were a few individuals rather than a set found this statement inadequate although it was abundantly difficult for them to explain their feeling. Such an Italian type frustrated by its setting in an unimpassioned and moral community was of necessity misinterpreted although its charm was valued. Mabel's ancestry did not supply any explanation of her character. Her kinship with decadent Italy was purely spiritual.

The capacity for composing herself with her room in unaccented and perfect values was the most complete attribute of that kinship that her modern environment had developed. As for the rest it after all amounted to failure, failure as power, failure as an individual. Her passions in spite of their intensity failed to take effective hold on the objects of her desire. The subtlety and impersonality of her atmosphere which in a position of recognised power would have had compelling attraction, here in a community of equals where there could be no mystery as the seeker had complete liberty in seeking she lacked the vital force necessary to win. Although she was unscrupulous the weapons she used were too brittle, they could always be broken in pieces by a vigorous guard.

Modern situations never endure for a long enough time to allow subtle and elaborate methods to succeed. By the time they are beginning to bring about results the incident is forgotten. Subtlety moreover in order to command efficient power must be realised as dangerous and the modern world is a difficult place in which to be subtly dangerous, the risks are too great. Mabel might now compel by inspiring pity, she could never in her world compel by inspiring fear.

Adele had been for some time one of Mabel's selected few. Her enjoyment of ease and her habit of infinite leisure, combined with her vigorous personality and a capacity for endless and picturesque analysis of all things human had established a claim which her instinct for intimacy without familiarity and her ready adjustment to the necessary impersonality which a relation with Mabel demanded, had confirmed.

"It's more or less of a bore getting back for we are all agreed that Baltimore isn't much of a town to live in, but this old habit is certainly very pleasant" she remarked as she stretched herself comfortably on the couch "and after all, it is much more possible to cultivate such joys when a town isn't wildly exciting. No my tea isn't quite right" she continued. "It's worth while making a fuss you know when there is a possibility of obtaining perfection, otherwise any old tea is good enough. Anyhow what's the use of anything as long as it isn't Spain? You must really go there some time." They continued to make the most of their recent experiences in this their first meeting.

"Did you stay long in New York after you landed?" Mabel finally asked. "Only a few days" Adele replied "I suppose Helen wrote you that I saw her for a little while. We lunched together before I took my train," she added with a consciousness of the embarrassment that that meeting had caused her. "You didn't expect to like her so much, did you?" Mabel suggested. "I remember you used to say that she impressed you as almost coarse and rather decadent and that you didn't even find her interesting. And you know" she added "how much you dislike decadence."

Adele met her with frank bravado. "Of course I said that and as yet I don't retract it. I am far from sure that she is not both coarse and decadent and I don't approve of either of those qualities. I do grant you however that she is interesting, at least as a character, her talk interests me no more than it ever did" and then facing the game more boldly, she continued "but you know I really know very little about her except that she dislikes her parents and goes in for society a good deal. What else is there?"

Mabel drew a very unpleasant picture of that parentage. Her description of the father a successful lawyer and judge, and an excessively brutal and at the same time small-minded man who exercised great ingenuity in making himself unpleasant was not alluring, nor that of the mother who was very religious and spent most of her time mourning that it was not Helen that had been taken instead of the others a girl and boy whom she remembered as sweet gentle children.

One day when Helen was a young girl she heard her mother say to the father "Isn't it sad that Helen should have been the one to be left."

Mabel described their attempts to break Helen's spirit and their anger at their lack of success. "And now" Mabel went on "they object to everything that she does, to her friends and to everything she is interested in. Mrs. T. always sides with her husband. Of course they are proud of her good looks, her cleverness and social success but she won't get married and she doesn't care to please the people her mother wants her to belong to. They don't dare to say anything to her now because she is so much better able to say things that hurt than they are."

"I suppose there is very little doubt that Helen can be uncommonly nasty when she wants to be," laughed Adele, "and if she isn't sensitive to other people's pain, a talent for being successful in bitter repartee might become a habit that would make her a most uncomfortable daughter. I believe I might condole with the elders if they were to confide their sorrows to me. By the way doesn't Helen address them the way children commonly do their parents, she always speaks of them as Mr. and Mrs. T." "Oh yes" Mabel explained, "they observe the usual forms."

"It's a queer game," Adele commented, "coming as I do from a community where all no matter how much they may quarrel and disagree have strong family affection and great respect for the ties of blood, I find it difficult to realise." "Yes there you come in with your middle-class ideals again" retorted Mabel.

She then lauded Helen's courage and daring. "Whenever there is any difficulty with the horses or anything dangerous to be done they always call in Helen. Her father is also very small-minded in money matters. He gives her so little and whenever anything happens to the carriage if she is out in it, he makes her pay and she has to get the money as best she can. Her courage never fails and that is what makes her father so bitter, that she never gives any sign of yielding and if she decides to do a thing she is perfectly reckless, nothing stops her."

"That sounds very awful" mocked Adele "not being my-self of an heroic breed, I don't somehow realise that type much outside of story-books. That sort of person in real life doesn't seem very real, but I guess it's alright. Helen has courage I don't doubt that."

Mabel then described Helen's remarkable endurance of pain. She fell from a haystack one day and broke her arm. After she got home, her father was so angry that he wouldn't for some time have it attended to and she faced him boldly to the end. "She never winces or complains no matter how much she is hurt," Mabel concluded. "Yes I can believe that" Adele answered thoughtfully.

Throughout the whole of Mabel's talk of Helen, there was an implication of ownership that Adele found singularly irritating. She supposed that Mabel had a right to it but in that thought she found little comfort.

As the winter advanced, Adele took frequent trips to New York. She always spent some of her time with Helen. For some undefined reason a convention of secrecy governed their relations. They seemed in this way to emphasise their intention of working the thing out completely between them. To Adele's consciousness the necessity of this secrecy was only apparent when they were together. She felt no obligation to conceal this relation from her friends.

They arranged their meetings in the museums or in the park and sometimes they varied it by lunching together and taking interminable walks in the long straight streets. Adele was always staying with relatives and friends and although there was no reason why Helen should not have come to see her there, something seemed somehow to serve as one. As for Helen's house it seemed tacitly agreed between them that they should not complicate the situation by any relations with Helen's family and so they continued their homeless wanderings.

Adele spent much of their time together in announcing with great interest the result of her endless meditations. She would criticise and examine herself and her ideas with tireless interest. "Helen," she said one day, "I always had an impression that you talked a great deal but apparently you are a most silent being. What is it? Do I talk so hopelessly much that you get discouraged with it as a habit?" "No," answered Helen, "although I admit one might look upon you in the light of a warning, but really I am very silent when I know people well. I only talk when I am with superficial acquaintances." Adele laughed. "I am tempted to say for the sake of picturesque effect, that in that respect I am your complete opposite, but honesty compels me to admit in myself an admirable consistency. I don't know that the quantity is much affected by any conditions in which I find myself, but really Helen why don't you talk more to me?" "Because you know well enough that you are not interested in my ideas, in fact that they bore you. It's always been very evident. You know" Helen continued affectionately, "that you haven't much talent for concealing your feelings and impressions." Adele smiled, "Yes you are certainly right about most of your talk, it does bore me," she admitted. "But that is because it's about stuff that you are not really interested in. You don't really care about general ideas and art values and musical development and surgical operations and Heaven knows what all and naturally your talk about those things doesn't interest me. No talking is interesting that one hasn't hammered out oneself. I know I always bore

myself unutterably when I talk the thoughts that I hammered out some time ago and that are no longer meaningful
to me, for quoting even oneself lacks a flavor of reality, but
you, you always make me feel that at no period did you ever
have the thoughts that you converse with. Surely one has to
hit you awfully hard to shake your realer things to the
surface."

These meetings soon became impossible. It was getting cold
and unpleasant and it obviously wouldn't do to continue in
that fashion and yet neither of them undertook to break the
convention of silence which they had so completely adopted
concerning the conditions of their relation.

One day after they had been lunching together they both
felt strongly that restaurants had ceased to be amusing.
They didn't want to stay there any longer but outside there
was an unpleasant wet snow-storm, it was dark and gloomy
and the streets were slushy. Helen had a sudden inspiration.
"Let us go and see Jane Fairfield," she said, "you don't
know her of course but that makes no difference. She is
queer and will interest you and you are queer and will interest her. Oh! I don't want to listen to your protests, you
are queer and interesting even if you don't know it and you
like queer and interesting people even if you think you don't
and you are not a bit bashful in spite of your convictions to
the contrary, so come along." Adele laughed and agreed.

They wandered up to the very top of an interminable New
York apartment house. It was one of the variety made up
apparently of an endless number of unfinished boxes of all
sizes piled up in a great oblong leaving an elevator shaft in

the centre. There is a strange effect of bare wood and un-
covered nails about these houses and no amount of up-
holstery really seems to cover their hollow nakedness.

Jane Fairfield was not at home but the elevator boy trust-
ingly let them in to wait. They looked out of the windows
at the city all gloomy and wet and white stretching down to
the river, and they watched the long tracks of the elevated
making such wonderful perspective that it never really
seemed to disappear, it just infinitely met.

Finally they sat down on the couch to give their hostess
just another quarter of an hour in which to return, and then
for the first time in Adele's experience something happened
in which she had no definite consciousness of beginnings.
She found herself at the end of a passionate embrace.

Some weeks after when Adele came again to New York they
agreed to meet at Helen's house. It had been arranged quite
as a matter of course as if no objection to such a proceeding
had ever been entertained. Adele laughed to herself as she
thought of it. "Why we didn't before and why we do now
are to me equally mysterious" she said shrugging her
shoulders. "Great is Allah, Mohammed is no Shodah!
though I dimly suspect that sometimes he is."

When the time came for keeping her engagement Adele
for some time delayed going and remained lying on her
friend's couch begging to be detained. She realised that her
certain hold on her own frank joyousness and happy serenity
was weakened. She almost longed to back out, she did so
dread emotional complexities. "Oh for peace and a quiet
life!" she groaned as she rang Helen's door-bell.

In Helen's room she found a note explaining that being

worried as it was so much past the hour of appointment, she had gone to the Museum as Adele had perhaps misunderstood the arrangement. If she came in she was to wait. "It was very bad of me to fool around so long" Adele said to herself gravely and then sat down very peacefully to read.

"I am awfully sorry" Adele greeted Helen as she came into the room somewhat intensely, "it never occurred to me that you would be bothered, it was just dilatoriness on my part," and then they sat down. After a while Helen came and sat on the arm of Adele's chair. She took her head between tense arms and sent deep into her eyes a long straight look of concentrated question. "Haven't you anything to say to me?" she asked at last. "Why no, nothing in particular," Adele answered slowly. She met Helen's glance for a moment, returned it with simple friendliness and then withdrew from it.

"You are very chivalrous," Helen said with sad self-defiance. "You realise that there ought to be shame somewhere between us and as I have none, you generously undertake it all." "No I am not chivalrous" Adele answered, "but I realise my deficiencies. I know that I always take an everlasting time to arrive anywhere really and that the rapidity of my superficial observation keeps it from being realised. It is certainly all my fault. I am so very deceptive. I arouse false expectations. You see," she continued meeting her again with pleasant friendliness, "you haven't yet learned that I am at once impetuous and slow-minded."

Time passed and they renewed their habit of desultory meetings at public places, but these were not the same as before. There was between them now a consciousness of strain, a sense of new adjustments, of uncertain standards and of changing values.

Helen was patient but occasionally moved to trenchant criticism, Adele was irritable and discursive but always ended with a frank almost bald apology for her inadequacy.

In the course of time they again arranged to meet in Helen's room. It was a wet rainy, sleety day and Adele felt chilly and unresponsive. Throwing off her hat and coat, she sat down after a cursory greeting and looked meditatively into the fire. "How completely we exemplify entirely different types" she began at last without looking at her companion. "You are a blooming Anglo-Saxon. You know what you want and you go and get it without spending your days and nights changing backwards and forwards from yes to no. If you want to stick a knife into a man you just naturally go and stick straight and hard. You would probably kill him but it would soon be over while I, I would have so many compunctions and considerations that I would cut up all his surface anatomy and make it a long drawn agony but unless he should bleed to death quite by accident, I wouldn't do him any serious injury. No you are the very brave man, passionate but not emotional, capable of great sacrifice but not tender-hearted.

"And then you really want things badly enough to go out and get them and that seems to me very strange. I want things too but only in order to understand them and I never go and get them. I am a hopeless coward, I hate to risk hurting myself or anybody else. All I want to do is to meditate endlessly and think and talk. I know you object because you believe it necessary to feel something to think about and you contend that I don't give myself time to find it. I recognise the justice of that criticism and I am doing my best these days to let it come."

She relapsed into silence and sat there smiling ironically into the fire. The silence grew longer and her smile turned into a look almost of disgust. Finally she wearily drew breath, shook her head and got up. "Ah! don't go," came from Helen in quick appeal. Adele answered the words. "No I am not going. I just want to look at these books." She wandered about a little. Finally she stopped by Helen's side and stood looking down at her with a gentle irony that wavered on the edge of scorn.

"Do you know" she began in her usual tone of dispassionate inquiry "you are a wonderful example of double personality. The you that I used to know and didn't like, and the occasional you that when I do catch a glimpse of it seems to me so very wonderful, haven't any possible connection with each other. It isn't as if my conception of you had gradually changed because it hasn't. I realise always one whole you consisting of a laugh so hard that it rattles, a voice that suggests a certain brutal coarseness and a point of view that is aggressively unsympathetic, and all that is one whole you and it alternates with another you that possesses a purity and intensity of feeling that leaves me quite awestruck and a gentleness of voice and manner and an infinitely tender patience that entirely overmasters me. Now the question is which is really you because these two don't seem to have any connections. Perhaps when I really know something about you, the whole will come together but at present it is always either the one or the other and I haven't the least idea which is reallest. You certainly are one too many for me." She shrugged her shoulders, threw out her hands helplessly and sat down again before the fire. She roused at last and became conscious that Helen was trembling bitterly. All hesitations were swept away by Adele's instant passionate sympathy for a creature obviously in pain and she took her into her arms with pure maternal tenderness. Helen gave way utterly. "I tried to be adequate to your experiments" she said at last "but you had no mercy. You were not content until you had dissected out every nerve in my body and left it quite exposed and it was too much, too much. You should give your subjects occasional respite even in the ardor of research." She said it without bitterness. "Good God" cried Adele utterly dumbfounded "did you think that I was deliberately making you suffer in order to study results? Heavens and earth what do you take me for! Do you suppose that I for a moment realised that you were in pain. No! no! it is only my cursed habit of being concerned only with my own thoughts, and then you know I never for a moment believed that you really cared about me, that is one of the things that with all my conceit I never can believe. Helen how could you have had any use for me if you thought me capable of such wanton cruelty?" "I didn't know," she answered "I was willing that you should do what you liked if it interested you and I would stand it as well as I could." "Oh! Oh!" groaned Adele yearning over her with remorseful sympathy "surely dear you believe that I had no idea of your pain and that my brutality was due to ignorance and not intention." "Yes! yes! I know" whispered Helen, nestling to her. After a while she went on, "You know dear you mean so very much to me for with all your inveterate egotism you are the only person with whom I have ever come into close contact, whom I could continue to respect."

"Faith" said Adele ruefully "I confess I can't see why. After all even at my best I am only tolerably decent. There are plenty of others, your experience has been unfortunate that's all, and then you know you have always shut yourself off by that fatal illusion of yours that you could stand completely alone." And then she chanted with tender mockery, "And the very strong man Kwasind and he was a very strong man" she went on "even if being an unconquerable solitary wasn't entirely a success."

## 2

All through the winter Helen at intervals spent a few days with Mabel Neathe in Baltimore. Adele was always more or less with them on these occasions. On the surface they preserved the same relations as had existed on the steamer. The only evidence that Mabel gave of a realisation of a difference was in never if she could avoid it leaving them alone together.

It was tacitly understood between them that on these rare occasions they should give each other no sign. As the time drew near when Adele was once more to leave for Europe this time for an extended absence, the tension of this self-imposed inhibition became unendurable and they as tacitly ceased to respect it.

Some weeks before her intended departure Adele was one afternoon as usual taking tea with Mabel. "You have never met Mr. and Mrs. T. have you?" Mabel asked quite out of the air. They had never definitely avoided talking of Helen but they had not spoken of her unnecessarily. "No" Adele answered, "I haven't wanted to. I don't like perfunctory civilities and I know that I belong to the number of Helen's friends of whom they do not approve." "You would not be burdened by their civility, they never take the trouble to be as amiable as that." "Are your experiences so very unpleasant when you are stopping there? I shouldn't think that you would care to do it often." "Sometimes I feel as if it couldn't be endured but if I didn't, Helen would leave them and I think she would regret that and so I don't want her to do it. I have only to say the word and she would leave them at once and sometimes I think she will do it anyway. If she once makes up her mind she won't reconsider it. Of course I wouldn't say such things to any one but you, you know." "I can quite believe that," said Adele rather grimly, "isn't there anything else that you would like to tell me just because I am I. If so don't let me get in your way." "I have never told you about our early relations," Mabel continued. "You know Helen cared for me long before I knew anything about it. We used to be together a great deal at College and every now and then she would disappear for a long time into the country and it wasn't until long afterwards that I found out the reason of it. You know Helen never gives way. You have no idea how wonderful she is. I have been so worried lately" she went on "lest she should think it necessary to leave home for my sake because it is so uncomfortable for me in the summer when I spend a month with her." "Well then why don't you make a noble sacrifice and stay away? Apparently Helen's heroism is great enough to carry her through the ordeal." Adele felt herself to be quite satisfactorily vulgar. Mabel accepted it literally. "Do you really advise it?" she asked. "Oh yes" said Adele "there is nothing so good for the soul as self-imposed periods of total abstinence." "Well,

I will think about it" Mabel answered "it is such a comfort that you understand everything and one can speak to you openly about it all." "That's where you are entirely mistaken" Adele said decisively, "I understand nothing. But after all" she added, "it isn't any of my business anyway. Adios," and she left.

When she got home she saw a letter of Helen's on the table. She felt no impulse to read it. She put it well away. "Not that it is any of my business whether she is bound and if so how," she said to herself. "That is entirely for her to work out with her own conscience. For me it is only a question of what exists between us two. I owe Mabel nothing"; and she resolutely relegated it all quite to the background of her mind.

Mabel however did not allow the subject to rest. At the very next opportunity she again asked Adele for advice. "Oh hang it all" Adele broke out "what do I know about it? I understand nothing of the nature of the bond between you." "Don't you really?" Mabel was seriously incredulous. "No I don't." Adele answered with decision, and the subject dropped.

Adele communed with herself dismally. "I was strong-minded to put it out of my head once, but this time apparently it has come to stay. I can't deny that I do badly want to know and I know well enough that if I continue to want to know the only decent thing for me to do is to ask the information of Helen. But I do so hate to do that. Why? well I suppose because it would hurt so to hear her admit that she was bound. It would be infinitely pleasanter to have Mabel explain it but it certainly would be very contemptible of me to get it from her. Helen is right, it's not easy this business of really caring about people. I seem to be pretty deeply in it" and she smiled to herself "because now I don't regret the bother and the pain. I wonder if I am really beginning to care" and she lost herself in a revery.

Mabel's room was now for Adele always filled with the atmosphere of the unasked question. She could dismiss it when alone but Mabel was clothed with it as with a garment although nothing concerning it passed between them.

Adele now received a letter from Helen asking why she had not written, whether it was that faith had again failed her. Adele at first found it impossible to answer; finally she wrote a note at once ambiguous and bitter.

At last the tension snapped. "Tell me then" Adele said to Mabel abruptly one evening. Mabel made no attempt to misunderstand but she did attempt to delay. "Oh well if you want to go through the farce of a refusal and an insistence, why help yourself," Adele broke out harshly, "but supposing all that done, I say again tell me." Mabel was dismayed by Adele's hot directness and she vaguely fluttered about as if to escape. "Drop your intricate delicacy" Adele said sternly "you wanted to tell, now tell." Mabel was cowed. She sat down and explained.

The room grew large and portentous and to Mabel's eyes Adele's figure grew almost dreadful in its concentrated repulsion. There was a long silence that seemed to roar and menace and Mabel grew afraid. "Good-night" said Adele and left her.

Adele had now at last learned to stop thinking. She went home and lay motionless a long time. At last she got up and sat at her desk. "I guess I must really care a good deal about

Helen" she said at last, "but oh Lord," she groaned and it was very bitter pain. Finally she roused herself. "Poor Mabel" she said "I could almost find it in my heart to be sorry for her. I must have looked very dreadful."

On the next few occasions nothing was said. Finally Mabel began again. "I really supposed Adele that you knew, or else I wouldn't have said anything about it at all and after I once mentioned it, you know you made me tell." "Oh yes I made you tell." Adele could admit it quite cheerfully; Mabel seemed so trivial. "And then you know," Mabel continued "I never would have mentioned it if I had not been so fond of you." Adele laughed, "Yes it's wonderful what an amount of devotion to me there is lying around the universe; but what will Helen think of the results of this devotion of yours?" "That is what worries me" Mabel admitted "I must tell her that I have told you and I am afraid she won't like it." "I rather suspect she won't" and Adele laughed again "but there is nothing like seizing an opportunity before your courage has a chance to ooze. Helen will be down next week, you know, and that will give you your chance but I guess now there has been enough said," and she definitely dismissed the matter.

Adele found it impossible to write to Helen, she felt too sore and bitter but even in spite of her intense revulsion of feeling, she realised that she did still believe in that other Helen that she had attempted once to describe to her. In spite of all evidence she was convinced that something real existed there, something that she was bound to reverence.

She spent a painful week struggling between revulsion and respect. Finally two days before Helen's visit, she heard from her. "I am afraid I can bear it no longer" Helen wrote.

"As long as I believed there was a chance of your learning to be something more than your petty complacent self, I could willingly endure everything, but now you remind me of an ignorant mob. You trample everything ruthlessly under your feet without considering whether or not you kill something precious and without being changed or influenced by what you so brutally destroy. I am like Diogenes in quest of an honest man; I want so badly to find some one I can respect and I find them all worthy of nothing but contempt. You have done your best. I am sorry."

For some time Adele was wholly possessed by hot anger, but that changed to intense sympathy for Helen's pain. She realised the torment she might be enduring and so sat down at once to answer. "Perhaps though she really no longer cares" she thought to herself and hesitated. "Well whether she does or not makes no difference I will at least do my part."

"I can make no defence" she wrote "except only that in spite of all my variations there has grown within me steadily an increasing respect and devotion to you. I am not surprised at your bitterness but your conclusions from it are not justified. It is hardly to be expected that such a changed estimate of values, such a complete departure from established convictions as I have lately undergone could take place without many revulsions. That you have been very patient I fully realise but on the other hand you should recognise that I too have done my best and your word to the contrary notwithstanding that best has not been contemptible. So don't talk any more nonsense about mobs. If your endurance is not equal to this task, why admit it and have done with it; if it is I will try to be adequate."

Adele knew that Helen would receive her letter but there would not be time to answer it as she was to arrive in Baltimore the following evening. They were all three to meet at the opera that night so for a whole day Adele would be uncertain of Helen's feeling toward her. She spent all her strength throughout the day in endeavoring to prepare herself to find that Helen still held her in contempt. It had always been her habit to force herself to realise the worst that was likely to befall her and to submit herself before the event. She was never content with simply thinking that the worst might happen and having said it to still expect the best, but she had always accustomed herself to bring her mind again and again to this worst possibility until she had really mastered herself to bear it. She did this because she always doubted her own courage and distrusted her capacity to meet a difficulty if she had not inured herself to it beforehand.

All through this day she struggled for her accustomed definite resignation and the tremendous difficulty of accomplishment made her keenly realise how much she valued Helen's regard.

She did not arrive at the opera until after it had commenced. She knew how little command she had of her expression when deeply moved and she preferred that the first greeting should take place in the dark. She came in quietly to her place. Helen leaned across Mabel and greeted her. There was nothing in her manner to indicate anything and Adele realised by her sensation of sick disappointment that she had really not prepared herself at all. Now that the necessity was more imperative she struggled again for resignation and by the time the act was over she had pretty well gained it. She had at least mastered herself enough to entertain Mabel with elaborate discussion of music and knife fights. She avoided noticing Helen but that was comparatively simple as Mabel sat between them.

*Carmen* that night was to her at once the longest and the shortest performance that she had ever sat through. It was short because the end brought her nearer to hopeless certainty. It was long because she could only fill it with suspense.

The opera was at last or already over, Adele was uncertain which phrase expressed her feeling most accurately, and then they went for a little while to Mabel's room. Adele was by this time convinced that all her relation with Helen was at an end.

"You look very tired to-night, what's the matter?" Mabel asked her. "Oh!" she explained "there's been a lot of packing and arranging and good-bys to say and farewell lunches and dinners to eat. How I hate baked shad, it's a particular delicacy now and I have lunched and dined on it for three days running so I think it's quite reasonable for me to be worn out. Good-by no don't come downstairs with me. Hullo Helen has started down already to do the honors. Good-by I will see you again to-morrow." Mabel went back to her room and Helen was already lost in the darkness of the lower hall. Adele slowly descended the stairs impressing herself with the necessity of self-restraint.

"Can you forgive me?" and Helen held her close. "I haven't anything to forgive if you still care," Adele answered. They were silent together a long time. "We will certainly have earned our friendship when it is finally accomplished," Adele said at last.

"Well good-by," Mabel began as the next day Adele was leaving for good. "Oh! before you go I want to tell you that it's alright. Helen was angry but it's alright now. You will be in New York for a few days before you sail" she continued. "I know you won't be gone for a whole year, you will be certain to come back to us before long. I will think of your advice" she concluded. "You know it carries so much weight coming from you." "Oh of course" answered Adele and thought to herself, "What sort of a fool does Mabel take me for anyway."

Adele was in Helen's room the eve of her departure. They had been together a long time. Adele was sitting on the floor her head resting against Helen's knee. She looked up at Helen and then broke the silence with some effort. "Before I go" she said "I want to tell you myself what I suppose you know already, that Mabel has told me of the relations existing between you." Helen's arms dropped away. "No I didn't know." She was very still. "Mabel didn't tell you then?" Adele asked. "No" replied Helen. There was a sombre silence. "If you were not wholly selfish, you would have exercised self-restraint enough to spare me this," Helen said. Adele hardly heard the words, but the power of the mood that possessed Helen awed her. She broke through it at last and began with slow resolution.

"I do not admit" she said, "that I was wrong in wanting to know. I suppose one might in a spirit of quixotic generosity deny oneself such a right but as a reasonable being, I feel that I had a right to know. I realise perfectly that it was hopelessly wrong to learn it from Mabel instead of from you. I admit I was a coward, I was simply afraid to ask you." Helen laughed harshly. "You need not have been," she said "I would have told you nothing." "I think you are wrong, I am quite sure that you would have told me and I wanted to spare myself that pain, perhaps spare you it too, I don't know. I repeat I cannot believe that I was wrong in wanting to know."

They remained there together in an unyielding silence. When an irresistible force meets an immovable body what happens? Nothing. The shadow of a long struggle inevitable as their different natures lay drearily upon them. This incident however decided was only the beginning. All that had gone before was only a preliminary. They had just gotten into position.

The silence was not oppressive but it lasted a long time. "I am very fond of you Adele" Helen said at last with a deep embrace.

It was an hour later when Adele drew a deep breath of resolution, "What foolish people those poets are who say that parting is such sweet sorrow. Although it isn't for ever I can't find a bit of sweetness in it not one tiny little speck. Helen I don't like at all this business of leaving you." "And I" Helen exclaimed "when in you I seem to be taking farewell of parents, brothers sisters my own child, everything at once. No dear you are quite right there is nothing pleasant in it."

"Then why do they put it into the books?" Adele asked with dismal petulance. "Oh dear! but at least it's some comfort to have found out that they are wrong. It's one fact discovered anyway. Dear we are neither of us sorry that we know enough to find it out, are we?" "No," Helen answered "we are neither of us sorry."

On the steamer Adele received a note of farewell from Mabel in which she again explained that nothing but her great regard for Adele would have made it possible for her to speak as she had done. Adele lost her temper. "I am willing to fight in any way that Mabel likes" she said to herself "underhand or overhand, in the dark, or in the light, in a room or out of doors but at this I protest. She unquestionably did that for a purpose even if the game was not successful. I don't blame her for the game, a weak man must fight with such weapons as he can hold but I don't owe it to her to endure the hypocrisy of a special affection. I can't under the circumstances be very straight but I'll not be unnecessarily crooked. I'll make it clear to her but I'll complicate it in the fashion that she loves."

"My dear Mabel" she wrote, "either you are duller than I would like to think you or you give me credit for more good-natured stupidity than I possess. If the first supposition is correct then you have nothing to say and I need say nothing; if the second then nothing that you would say would carry weight so it is equally unnecessary for you to say anything. If you don't understand what I am talking about then I am talking about nothing and it makes no difference, if you do then there's enough said." Mabel did not answer for several months and then began again to write friendly letters.

It seemed incredible to Adele this summer that it was only one year ago that she had seemed to herself so simple and all morality so easily reducible to formula. In these long lazy Italian days she did not discuss these matters with herself. She realised that at present morally and mentally she was too complex, and that complexity too much astir. It would take much time and strength to make it all settle again. It might, she thought, be eventually understood, it might even in a great deal of time again become simple but at present it gave little promise.

She poured herself out fully and freely to Helen in their ardent correspondence. At first she had had some hesitation about this. She knew that Helen and Mabel were to be together the greater part of the summer and she thought it possible that both the quantity and the matter of the correspondence, if it should come to Mabel's notice would give Helen a great deal of bother. She hesitated a long time whether to suggest this to Helen and to let her decide as to the expediency of being more guarded.

There were many reasons for not mentioning the matter. She realised that not alone Helen but that she herself was still uncertain as to the fidelity of her own feeling. She could not as yet trust herself and hesitated to leave herself alone with a possible relapse.

"After all," she said to herself, "it is Helen's affair and not mine. I have undertaken to follow her lead even into very devious and underground ways but I don't know that it is necessary for me to warn her. She knows Mabel as well as I do. Perhaps she really won't be sorry if the thing is brought to a head."

She remembered the reluctance that Helen always showed to taking precautions or to making any explicit statement of conditions. She seemed to satisfy her conscience and keep herself from all sense of wrong-doing by never allowing herself to expect a difficulty. When it actually arrived the active necessity of using whatever deception was necessary to cover it, drowned her conscience in the violence of action. Adele did not as yet realise this quality definitely but she was vaguely aware that Helen would shut her mind to any explicit statement of probabilities, that she would take no precautions and would thus avoid all sense of guilt. In this fashion she could safeguard herself from her own conscience.

Adele recognised all this dimly. She did not formulate it but it aided to keep her from making any statement to Helen.

She herself could not so avoid her conscience, she simply had to admit a change in moral basis. She knew what she was doing, she realised what was likely to happen and the way in which the new developments would have to be met.

She acknowledged to herself that her own defence lay simply in the fact that she thought the game was worth the candle. "After all" she concluded, "there is still the most important reason for saying nothing. The stopping of the correspondence would make me very sad and lonely. In other words I simply don't want to stop it and so I guess I won't."

For several months the correspondence continued with vigor and ardour on both sides. Then there came a three weeks' interval and no word from Helen then a simple friendly letter and then another long silence.

Adele lying on the green earth on a sunny English hillside communed with herself on these matters day after day. She had no real misgiving but she was deeply unhappy. Her unhappiness was the unhappiness of loneliness not of doubt. She saved herself from intense misery only by realising that the sky was still so blue and the country-side so green and beautiful. The pain of passionate longing was very hard to bear. Again and again she would bury her face in the cool grass to recover the sense of life in the midst of her sick despondency.

"There are many possibilities but to me only one proba- bility," she said to herself. "I am not a trustful person in spite of an optimistic temperament but I am absolutely cer- tain in the face of all the facts that Helen is unchanged. Unquestionably there has been some complication. Mabel has gotten hold of some letters and there has been trouble. I can't blame Mabel much. The point of honor would be a difficult one to decide between the three of us."

As time passed she did not doubt Helen but she began to be much troubled about her responsibility in the matter. She felt uncertain as to the attitude she should take.

"As for Mabel" she said to herself "I admit quite com- pletely that I simply don't care. I owe her nothing. She wanted me when it was pleasant to have me and so we are quits. She entered the fight and must be ready to bear the results. We were never bound to each other, we never trusted each other and so there has been no breach of faith. She would show me no mercy and I need grant her none, particularly as she would wholly misunderstand it. It is very strange how very different one's morality and one's temper are when one wants something really badly. Here I, who have always been hopelessly soft-hearted and good-natured and who have always really preferred letting the other man win, find myself quite cold-blooded and relentless. It's a lovely morality that in which we believe even in serious mat- ters when we are not deeply stirred, it's so delightfully noble and gentle." She sighed and then laughed. "Well, I hope some day to find a morality that can stand the wear and tear of real desire to take the place of the nice one that I have lost, but morality or no morality the fact remains that I have no compunctions on the score of Mabel.

"About Helen that's a very different matter. I unquestionably do owe her a great deal but just how to pay it is the difficult point to discover. I can't forget that to me she can never be the first consideration as she is to Mabel for I have other claims that I would always recognise as more important. I have neither the inclination or the power to take Mabel's place and I feel therefore that I have no right to step in between them. On the other hand morally and mentally she is in urgent need of a strong comrade and such in spite of all evidence I believe myself to be. Some day if we continue she will in spite of herself be compelled to choose between us and what have I to offer? Nothing but an elevating influence.

"Bah! what is the use of an elevating influence if one hasn't bread and butter. Her possible want of butter if not of bread, considering her dubious relations with her family must be kept in mind. Mabel could and would always supply them and I neither can nor will. Alas for an unbuttered influence say I. What a grovelling human I am anyway. But I do have occasional sparkling glimpses of faith and those when they come I truly believe to be worth much bread and butter. Perhaps Helen also finds them more delectable. Well I will state the case to her and abide by her decision."

She timed her letter to arrive when Helen would be once more at home alone. "I can say to you now" she wrote "what I found impossible in the early summer. I am now convinced and I think you are too that my feeling for you is genuine and loyal and whatever may be our future difficulties we are now at least on a basis of understanding and trust. I know therefore that you will not misunderstand when I beg you to consider carefully whether on the whole you had not better give me up. I can really amount to so little for you and yet will inevitably cause you so much trouble. That I dread your giving me up I do not deny but I dread more being the cause of serious annoyance to you. Please believe that this statement is sincere and is to be taken quite literally."

"Hush little one" Helen answered "oh you stupid child, don't you realise that you are the only thing in the world that makes anything seem real or worth while to me. I have had a dreadful time this summer. Mabel read a letter of mine to you and it upset her completely. She said that she found it but I can hardly believe that. She asked me if you cared for me and I told her that I didn't know and I really don't dearest. She did not ask me if I cared for you. The thing upset her completely and she was jealous of my every thought and I could not find a moment even to feel alone with you. But don't please don't say any more about giving you up. You are not any trouble to me if you will only not leave me. It's alright now with Mabel, she says that she will never be jealous again." "Oh Lord!" groaned Adele "well if she isn't she would be a hopeless fool. Anyhow I said I would abide by Helen's decision and I certainly will but how so proud a woman can permit such control is more than I can understand."

# Book 3: HELEN

## 1

THERE IS NO PASSION more dominant and instinctive in
the human spirit than the need of the country to which one
belongs. One often speaks of homesickness as if in its intense form it were the peculiar property of Swiss moun-
taineers, Scandinavians, Frenchmen and those other nations
that too have a poetic background, but poetry is no element
in the case. It is simply a vital need for the particular air that
is native, whether it is the used up atmosphere of London,
the clean-cut cold of America or the rarefied air of Swiss
mountains. The time comes when nothing in the world is so
important as a breath of one's own particular climate. If it
were one's last penny it would be used for that return
passage.

An American in the winter fogs of London can realise this
passionate need, this desperate longing in all its completeness. The dead weight of that fog and smoke laden air, the
sky that never suggests for a moment the clean blue distance

that has been the accustomed daily comrade, the dreary sun, moon and stars that look like painted imitations on the ceiling of a smoke-filled room, the soggy, damp, miserable streets, and the women with bedraggled, frayed-out skirts, their faces swollen and pimply with sordid dirt ground into them until it has become a natural part of their ugly surface all become day after day a more dreary weight of hopeless oppression.

A hopeful spirit resists. It feels that it must be better soon, it cannot last so forever; this afternoon, to-morrow this dead weight must lift, one must soon again realise a breath of clean air, but day after day the whole weight of fog, smoke and low brutal humanity rests a weary load on the head and back and one loses the power of straightening the body to actively bear the burden, it becomes simply a despairing endurance.

Just escaped from this oppresion, Adele stood in the saloon of an ocean steamer looking at the white snow line of New York harbor. A little girl one of a family who had also fled from England after a six months trial, stood next to her. They stayed side by side their faces close to the glass. A government ship passed flying the flag. The little girl looked deeply at it and then with slow intensity said quite to herself, "There is the American flag, it looks good." Adele echoed it, there was all America and it looked good; the clean sky and the white snow and the straight plain ungainly buildings all in a cold and brilliant air without spot or stain.

Adele's return had been unexpected and she landed quite alone. "No it wasn't to see you much as I wanted you," she explained to Helen long afterwards, "it was just plain America. I landed quite alone as I had not had time to let any of my friends know of my arrival but I really wasn't in a hurry to go to them much as I had longed for them all. I simply rejoiced in the New York streets, in the long spindling legs of the elevated, in the straight high undecorated houses, in the empty upper air and in the white surface of the snow. It was such a joy to realise that the whole thing was without mystery and without complexity, that it was clean and straight and meagre and hard and white and high. Much as I wanted you I was not eager for after all you meant to me a turgid and complex world, difficult yet necessary to understand and for the moment I wanted to escape all that, I longed only for obvious, superficial, clean simplicity."

Obeying this need Adele after a week of New York went to Boston. She steeped herself in the very essence of clear eyed Americanism. For days she wandered about the Boston streets rejoicing in the passionless intelligence of the faces. She revelled in the American street-car crowd with its ready intercourse, free comments and airy persiflage all without double meanings which created an atmosphere that never suggested for a moment the need to be on guard.

It was a cleanliness that began far inside of these people and was kept persistently washed by a constant current of clean cold water. Perhaps the weight of stains necessary to the deepest understanding might be washed away, it might well be that it was not earthy enough to be completely satisfying, but it was a delicious draught to a throat choked with soot and fog.

For a month Adele bathed herself in this cleanliness and then she returned to New York eager again for a world of greater complexity.

For some time after her return a certain estrangement

existed between Helen and herself. Helen had been much hurt at her long voluntary absence and Adele as yet did not sufficiently understand her own motives to be able to explain. It had seemed to her only that she rather dreaded losing herself again with Helen.

This feeling between them gradually disappeared. In their long sessions in Helen's room, Adele now too cultivated the habit of silent intimacy. As time went on her fear of Helen and of herself gradually died away and she yielded herself to the complete joy of simply being together.

One day they agreed between them that they were very near the state of perfect happiness. "Yes I guess it's alright" Adele said with a fond laugh "and when it's alright it certainly is very good. Am I not a promising pupil?" she asked. "Not nearly so good a pupil as so excellent a teacher as I am deserves" Helen replied. "Oh! Oh!" cried Adele, "I never realised it before but compared with you I am a model of humility. There is nothing like meeting with real arrogance. It makes one recognise a hitherto hidden virtue," and then they once more lost themselves in happiness.

It was a very real oblivion. Adele was aroused from it by a kiss that seemed to scale the very walls of chastity. She flung away on the instant filled with battle and revulsion. Utterly regardless of Helen she lay her face buried in her hands. "I never dreamed that after all that has come I was still such a virgin soul" she said to herself, "and that like Parsifal a kiss could make me frantic with realisation" and then she lost herself in the full tide of her fierce disgust.

She lay long in this new oblivion. At last she turned. Helen lay very still but on her face were bitter tears. Adele with her usual reaction of repentance tried to comfort. "Forgive me!'' she said "I don't know what possessed me. No you didn't do anything it was all my fault." "And we were so happy" Helen said. After a long silence she asked "Was it that you felt your old distrust of me again?" "Yes," replied Adele briefly. "I am afraid I can't forgive this," Helen said. "I didn't suppose that you could," Adele replied.

They continued to meet but each one was filled with her own struggle. Adele finally reopened the subject. "You see" she explained "my whole trouble lies in the fact that I don't know on what ground I am objecting, whether it is morality or a meaingless instinct. You know I have always had a conviction that no amount of reasoning will help in deciding what is right and possible for one to do. If you don't begin with some theory of obligation, anything is possible and no rule of right and wrong holds. One must either accept some theory or else believe one's instinct or follow the world's opinion.

"Now I have no theory and much as I would like to, I can't really regard the world's opinion. As for my instincts they have always been opposed to the indulgence of any feeling of passion. I suppose that is due to the Calvinistic influence that dominates American training and has interfered with my natural temperament. Somehow you have made me realise that my attitude in the matter was degradıng and material, instead of moral and spiritual but in spite of you my puritan instincts again and again say no and I get into a horrible mess. I am beginning to distrust my instincts and I am about convinced that my objection was not a deeply moral one. I suppose after all it was a good deal cowardice. Anyhow" she concluded, "I guess I haven't any moral objection any more and now if I have lost my instincts it will be alright and we can begin a new deal." "I am afraid I can't help you much" Helen answered "I can only hold by the fact that whatever you do and however much you hurt me I seem to have faith in you, in spite of yourself." Adele groaned. "How hopelessly inadequate I am," she said.

This completeness of revulsion never occurred again, but a new opposition gradually arose between them. Adele realised that Helen demanded of her a response and always before that response was ready. Their pulses were differently timed. She could not go so fast and Helen's exhausted nerves could no longer wait. Adele found herself constantly forced on by Helen's pain. She went farther than she could in honesty because she was unable to refuse anything to one who had given all. It was a false position. All reactions had now to be concealed as it was evident that Helen could no longer support that struggle. Their old openness was no longer possible and Adele ceased to express herself freely.

She realised that her attitude was misunderstood and that Helen interpreted her slowness as essential deficiency. This was the inevitable result of a situation in which she was forced constantly ahead of herself. She was sore and uneasy and the greater her affection for Helen became the more irritable became her discontent.

One evening they had agreed to meet at a restaurant and dine before going to Helen's room. Adele arriving a half hour late found Helen in a state of great excitement. "Why what's the matter?" Adele asked. "Matter" Helen repeated "you kept me waiting for you and a man came in and spoke to me and it's the first time that I have ever been so insulted." Adele gazed at her in astonishment. "Great guns!" she exclaimed "what do you expect if you go out alone at night. You must be willing to accept the consequences. The men are quite within their rights." "Their rights! They have no right to insult me." Adele shook her head in slow wonderment. "Will we ever understand each other's point of view," she said. "A thing that seems to unworldly, unheroic me so simple and inevitable and which I face quietly a score of times seems to utterly unnerve you while on the other hand,—but then we won't go into that, have something to eat and you will feel more cheerful."

"If you had been much later," Helen said as they were walking home, "I would have left and never have had anything farther to do with you until you apologised." "Bah!" exclaimed Adele. "I haven't any objection to apologising, the only thing I object to is being in the wrong. You are quite like a storybook" she continued, "you still believe in the divine right of heroics and of ladies. You think there is some higher power that makes the lower world tremble, when you say, 'Man how dare you!' That's all very well when the other man wants to be scared but when he doesn't it's the strongest man that wins."

They had been together for some time in the room, when Helen broke the silence. "I wonder," she said, "why I am doomed always to care for people who are so hopelessly inadequate." Adele looked at her a few moments and then wandered about the room. She returned to her seat, her face very still and set. "Oh! I didn't mean anything" said Helen, "I was only thinking about it all." Adele made no reply. "I think you might be patient with me when I am nervous and tired" Helen continued petulantly "and not be angry at everything I say." "I could be patient enough if I didn't think that you really meant what you have said," Adele answered. "I don't care what you say, the trouble is that you do believe it." "But you have said it yourself again and again" Helen complained. "That is perfectly true" returned Adele "but it is right for me to say it and to believe it too, but not for you. If you believe it, it puts a different face on the whole matter. It makes the situation intolerable." They were silent, Helen nervous and uneasy, and Adele rigid and quiet. "Oh why can't you forget it?" Helen cried at last. Adele roused herself. "It's alright" she said "don't bother. You are all tired out, come lie down and go to sleep." She remained with her a little while and then went into another room to read. She was roused from an unpleasant revery by Helen's sudden entrance. "I had such a horrible dream" she said "I thought that you were angry and had left me never to come back. Don't go away, please stay with me."

"You haven't forgiven me yet?" Helen asked the next morning as Adele was about to leave her. "It isn't a question of forgiveness, it's a question of your feeling," Adele replied steadily. "You have given no indication as yet that you did not believe what you said last night." "I don't know what I said," Helen evaded "I am worried and pestered and bothered and you just make everything harder for me and then accuse me of saying things that I shouldn't. Well perhaps I shouldn't have said it." "But nevertheless you believe it," Adele returned stubbornly. "Oh I don't know what I believe. I am so torn and bothered, can't you leave me alone?" "You have no right to constantly use your pain as a weapon!" Adele flashed out angrily. "What do you mean by that?" Helen demanded. "I mean that you force me on by your pain and then hold me responsible for the whole business. I am willing to stand for my own trouble but I will not endure the whole responsibility of yours." "Well aren't you responsible?" asked Helen, "have I done anything but be passive while you did as you pleased? I have been willing to endure it all, but I have not taken one step to hold you." Adele stared at her. "So that's your version of the situation is it? Oh well then there is no use in saying another word." She started to go and then stood irresolutely by the door. Helen dropped her head on her arms. Adele returned and remained looking down at her stubborn and unhappy. "Oh I shall go mad," Helen moaned. Adele stood motionless. Helen's hand dropped and Adele kneeling beside her took her into her arms with intense fondness, but they both realised that neither of them had yielded.

They were each too fond of the other ever to venture on an ultimatum for they realised that they would not be constant to it. The question of relative values and responsibilities was not again openly discussed between them. Subtly perhaps unconsciously but nevertheless persistently Helen now threw the burden of choice upon Adele. Just how it came about she never quite realised but inevitably now it was always Adele that had to begin and had to ask for the next meeting. Helen's attitude became that of one anxious to give all but unfortunately prevented by time and circumstances. Adele was sure that it was not that Helen had ceased to care but that intentionally or not she was nevertheless taking full advantage of the fact that Adele now cared equally as much.

Adele chafed under this new dispensation but nevertheless realised that it was no more than justice. In fact her submission went deeper. On the night of their quarrel she had realised for the first time Helen's understanding of what their relations had been and she now spent many weary nights in endeavoring to decide whether that interpretation was just and if she really was to that degree responsible. As time went on she became hopelessly confused and unhappy about the whole matter.

One night she was lying on her bed gloomy and disconsolate. Suddenly she burst out, "No I am not a cad. Helen has come very near to persuading me that I am but I really am not. We both went into this with our eyes open, and Helen fully as deliberately as myself. I never intentionally made her suffer however much she may think I did. No if one goes in, one must be willing to stand for the whole game and take the full responsibility of their own share."

"You know I don't understand your attitude at all," Adele said to Helen the next day. "I am thinking of your indignation at those men speaking to you that night when we had the quarrel. It seems to me one must be prepared to stand not only the actual results of one's acts but also all the implications of them. People of your heroic kind consider yourselves heroes when you are doing no more than the rest of us who look upon it only as humbly submitting to inevitable necessity." "What do you mean?" asked Helen. "Why simply that when one goes out of bounds one has no claim to righteous indignation if one is caught." "That depends somewhat on the method of going," answered Helen, "one can go out of bounds in such a manner that one's right must be respected." "One's right to do wrong?" Adele asked. "No for when it is done so it isn't wrong. You have not yet learned that things are not separated by such hard and fast lines, but I understand your meaning. You object because I have stopped enduring everything from you. You have no understanding of all that I have forgiven." "I have said it in fun and now I say it in earnest," Adele answered angrily "you are too hopelessly arrogant. Are you the only one that has had to endure and forgive?" "Oh yes I suppose that you think that you too have made serious sacrifices but I tell you that I never realised what complete scorn I was capable of feeling as that night when I kissed you and you flung me off in that fashion because you didn't know what it was that you wanted." "You are intolerable" Adele answered fiercely, "I at least realise that I am not always in the right, but you, you are incapable of understanding anything except your own point of view, or realising even distantly the value of a humility which acknowledges an error." "Humility" Helen repeated, "that is a strange claim for you to make for yourself." "May be," Adele answered "all things are relative. I never realised my virtue until it was brought out by contrast." "Oh I could be humble too," Helen retorted "if I could see any one who had made good a superior claim, but that hasn't come yet." "No, and with your native blindness it isn't likely that it ever will, that's quite true." "No it isn't blindness, it's because I understand values before I act on them. Oh yes I know you are generous enough after you have gone home and have had time to think it over, but it's the generosity of instinctive acts that counts and as to that I don't think there is much doubt as to who is the better man." "As you will!" cried Adele bursting violently from her chair with a thundering imprecation and then with the same movement and a feeling of infinite tenderness and sorrow she took Helen into her arms and kissed her. "What a great goose you are," said Helen fondly. "Oh yes I know it" Adele answered drearily, "but it's no use I can't remain angry even for one long moment. Repentance comes too swiftly but nevertheless I have a hopelessly persistent mind and after the pressure is removed I return to the old refrain. Dear don't forget, you really are in the wrong."

In spite of this outburst of reconciliation, things did not really improve between them. Helen still pursued her method of granting in inverse ratio to the strength of Adele's desire, and Adele's unhappiness and inward resistance grew steadily with the increase of her affection.

Before long the old problem of Mabel's claims further complicated the situation. "I am going abroad this summer again with Mabel," Helen said one day. Adele made no comment but the question "At whose expense?" was insistently in her mind.

In spite of the conviction that she owed Mabel nothing, she had had an uneasy sense concerning her during the whole winter. She had avoided going to Boston again as she did not wish to see her. She realised a sense of shame at the thought of meeting her. In spite of the clearness of her reasoning, she could not get rid of the feeling that she had stolen the property of another.

On the few occasions when the matter was spoken of between them, Helen while claiming her right to act as she pleased, admitted the validity of Mabel's claim. She declared repeatedly that in the extreme case if she had to give up some one it would be Adele and not Mabel, as Mabel would be unable to endure it, and Adele and herself were strong enough to support such a trial.

Just how Helen reconciled these conflicting convictions, Adele did not understand but as her own reconcilements were far from convincing to herself, she could ask for no explanations of the other's conscience. This statement of a foreign trip, probably at Mabel's expense made her once more face the situation. She had a strong sense of the sanctity of money obligations. She recognised as paramount the necessary return for value received in all cash considerations. Perhaps Helen had her own money but of this Adele was exceedingly doubtful. She wanted badly to know but she admitted to herself that this question she dared not ask.

The recognition of Helen's willingness to accept this of Mabel brought her some comfort. She lost her own sense of shame toward Mabel. "After all" she thought, "I haven't really robbed her of anything. She will win out eventually so I can meet her with a clearer conscience." She then told Helen that she intended going to Boston for a week before her return to Europe. Helen said nothing but it was evident that she did not wish her to go.

In this last month together there was less openness and confidence between them than at any time in their whole relation. Helen seemed content and indifferent but yet persisted always in answer to any statement of doubt from Adele that she was quite unchanged. Adele felt that her own distrust, stubbornness and affection were all steadily increasing. She deeply resented Helen's present attitude which was that of one granting all and more than all to a discontented petitioner. She felt Helen's continued statement of the sacrifices that she was making and even then the impossibility of satisfying her as both untruthful and insulting, but the conditions between them had become such that no explanations were possible.

Helen's attitude was now a triumph of passivity. Adele was forced to accept it with what grace she might. Her only consolation lay in the satisfaction to her pride in realising Helen's inadequacy in a real trial of generosity. When together now they seemed quite to have changed places. Helen was irritating and unsatisfying, Adele patient and for-bearing.

"I wonder if we will see each other in Italy" Adele said one day. "I certainly very much hope so" answered Helen. "It is only a little over a week and then I go to Boston and then I will be in New York only a few days before I sail," continued Adele, "when will I see you?" "On Monday eve-ning" suggested Helen. "Good" agreed Adele.

On Monday morning Adele received a note from Helen explaining that the arrival of a friend made it impossible for her to see her alone before the end of the week but she would be glad if she would join them at lunch. Adele was deeply hurt and filled with bitter resentment. She understood Helen's intention whether conscious or not in this delay. The realisation that in order to accomplish her ends Helen would not hesitate to cause her any amount of pain gave her a sense of sick despondency. She wrote a brief note saying that she did not think her presence at this lunch would tend greatly to the gayety of nations but that she would be at home in the evening if Helen cared to come. She got a hur-ried reply full of urgent protest but still holding to the original plan. "I guess this is the end of the story," Adele said to herself.

"The situation seems utterly hopeless" she wrote, "we

are more completely unsympathetic and understand each other less than at any time in our whole acquaintance. It may be my fault but nevertheless I find your attitude intolerable. You need feel no uneasiness about my going to Boston. I will not cause any trouble and as for the past I realise that as a matter of fact I have in no way interfered as you both still have all that is really vital to you."

"I guess that settles it," she said drearily as she dropped the letter into the mail-box. Helen made no sign. The days passed very quickly for Adele. All her actual consciousness found the definite ending of the situation a great relief. As long as one is firmly grasping the nettles there is no sting. The bitter pain begins when the hold begins to relax. At the actual moment of a calamity the undercurrents of pain, repentance and vain regret are buried deep under the ruins of the falling buildings and it is only when the whole mass begins to settle that they begin to well up here and there and at last rush out in an overwhelming flood of bitter pain. Adele in these first days that passed so quickly was peaceful and almost content. It was almost the end of the week when walking down town one day she saw Helen in the distance. It gave her a sudden shock and at first she was dazed but not moved by it, but gradually she became entirely possessed by the passion of her own longing and the pity of Helen's possible pain. Without giving herself time for consideration she wrote to her and told her that having seen her she had realised the intensity of her own affection but that she did not feel that she had been in the wrong either in feeling or expressing resentment but that if Helen cared to come, she would be at home in the morning to see her. "Certainly I will come," Helen answered.

When they met they tried to cover their embarrassment with commonplaces. Suddenly Adele frankly gave it up and went to the window and stared bravely out at the trees. Helen left standing in the room fought it out, finally she yielded and came to the window.

There was no ardor in their reconciliation, they had both wandered too far. Gradually they came together more freely but even then there was no openness of explanation between them. "As long as you have a soreness within that you don't express, nothing can be right between us," Helen said but to this appeal Adele could not make an open answer. There were things in her mind which she knew absolutely that Helen would not endure to hear spoken and so they could meet in mutual fondness but not in mutual honesty.

"Your letter upset me rather badly," Helen said some hours later. "In fact I am rather afraid I fainted." "But you would not have said a word to me, no matter how much you knew I longed for it?" Adele asked. "No" answered Helen "how could I?" "We are both proud women," Adele said "but mine doesn't take that form. As long as I thought there was a possibility of your caring, no amount of pain or humiliation would keep me from coming to you. But you do realise don't you," she asked earnestly "that however badly I may behave or whatever I may say or do my devotion and loyalty to you are absolute?" "Yes" answered Helen "I know it. I have learned my lesson too and I do trust you always." They both realised this clearly, Adele had learned to love and Helen to trust but still there was no real peace between them.

"Don't worry about me, I won't get into any trouble in Boston" Adele said cheerily as they parted. "You come back on Sunday?" Helen asked. "Yes and will see you Sunday evening and then only a few days and then I will be on the ocean. Unless we Marconi to each other we will then for some little time be unable to get into difficulties."

From Boston Adele wrote a letter to Helen full of nonsense and affection. She received just before her return a curt and distant answer.

"Well now what's gone wrong" she said impatiently, "will there never be any peace?"

When she arrived at Helen's room Sunday evening, Helen had not yet returned. She sat down and waited impatiently. Helen came in after a while radiant and cordial but very unfamiliar. Adele quietly watched her. Helen moved about and talked constantly. Adele was unresponsive and looked at her quite stolidly. At last Helen became quiet. Adele looked at her some time longer and then laughed. "Aren't you ashamed of yourself?" she asked. Helen made an effort to be heroic but failed. "Yes I am" she admitted "but your letter was so cocky and you had caused me so much trouble that I couldn't resist that temptation. There yes I am ashamed but it comes hard for me to say it." Adele laughed joyously. "Well it's the first and probably the last time in your history that you have ever realised your wrong-doing so let's celebrate" and there was peace between them.

It was not however a peace of long duration for soon it had all come back. Helen was once more inscrutable and Adele resentful and unhappy.

Adele was to sail on the next day and they were spending this last morning together. Adele was bitterly unhappy at the uncertainty of it all and Helen quite peaceful and content. Adele to conceal her feelings wandered up to a bookcase and began to read. She stuck to it resolutely until Helen, annoyed, came up to her. "Pshaw" she said "why do you spend our last morning together in this fashion?" "Because I am considerably unhappy," Adele replied. "Well you had better do as I do, wait to be unhappy until after you are gone," Helen answered. Adele remembered their parting a year ago when Helen's point of view had been different. "I might reply" she began, "but then I guess I won't" she added. "That I won't be unhappy even then, were you going to say?" Helen asked. "No I wasn't going to be quite as obvious as that," Adele answered and then wandered disconsolately about the room. She came back finally and sat on the arm of Helen's chair but held herself drearily aloof. "Why do you draw away from me, when you are unhappy?" Helen finally burst out. "Don't you trust me at all?"

A little later Adele was about to leave. They were standing at the door looking intently at each other. "Do you really care for me any more?" Adele asked at last. Helen was angry and her arms dropped. "You are impossible" she answered. "I have never before in my life ever given anybody more than one chance, and you, you have had seventy times seven and are no better than at first." She kissed her resignedly. "You have succeeded in killing me" she said drearily, "and now you are doing your best to kill yourself. Good-by I will come to see you this evening for a little while."

In the evening they began to discuss a possible meeting in Italy. "If I meet you there" Adele explained "I must do it deliberately for in the natural course of things I would be in France as my brother does not intend going South this summer. It's a question that you absolutely must decide. There is no reason why I should not come except only as it would please or displease you. As for Mabel she knows that I am fond of you and so it isn't necessary for me to conceal my emotions. It is only a question of you and your desires. You can't leave it to me" she concluded, "for you know, I have no power of resisting temptation, but I am strong enough to do as you say, so you must settle it." "I can certainly conceal my emotions so it would be perfectly safe even if you can't," answered Helen. "I am afraid though I haven't any more power of resisting temptation than you but I will think it over." Just as they parted Helen decided. "I think dear that you had better come" she said. "Alright" answered Adele.

## 2

There was nothing to distinguish Mabel Neathe and Helen Thomas from the average American woman tourist as they walked down the Via Nazionale. Their shirt-waists trimly pinned down, their veils depending in graceless folds from their hats, the little bags with the steel chain firmly grasped in the left hand, the straightness of their backs and the determination of their observation all marked them an integral part of that national sisterhood which shows a more uncompromising family likeness than a continental group of sisters with all their dresses made exactly alike.

This general American sisterhood has a deeper conformity than the specific European, because in the American it is a conformity from within out. They all look alike not because they want to or because they are forced to do it, but simply because they lack individual imagination.

The European sisterhood conform to a common standard

for economy or because it is a tradition to which they must submit but there is always the pathetic attempt to assert individual feeling in the difference of embroidery on a collar, or in a variation in tying of a bow and sometimes in the very daring by a different flower in the hat.

These two Americans then were like all the others. There was the same want of abundant life, the same inwardly compelled restrained movement, which kept them aloof from the life about them and the same intensely serious but unenthusiastic interest in the things to be observed. It was the walking of a dutiful purpose full of the necessity of observing many things among an alien mass of earthy spontaneity whose ideal expression is enthusiasm.

Behind them out of a side street came a young woman, the cut of whose shirt-waist alone betrayed her American origin. Large, abundant, full-busted and joyous, she seemed a part of the rich Roman life. She moved happily along, her white Panama hat well back on her head and an answering smile on her face as she caught the amused glances that fell upon her. Seeing the two in front she broke into a run, clapped them on the shoulder and as they turned with a start, she gave the national greeting "Hullo."

"Why Adele" exclaimed Helen, "where did you come from? You look as brown and white and clean as if you had just sprung out of the sea." With that they all walked on together. Adele kept up a lively talk with Mabel until they came to the pilgrimage church of the Santa Maria Maggiore. In the shelter of that great friendly hall she exchanged a word with Helen. "How are things going?" she asked. "Very badly" Helen replied.

They wandered about all together for a while and then

they agreed to take a drive out into the Campagna. They were all keenly conscious of the fact that this combination of themselves all together was most undesirable but this feeling was covered by an enthusiastic and almost convincing friendly spontaneity, and indeed the spontaneity and the friendliness were not forced or hypocritical for if it had not been that they all wanted something else so much more they would have had great enjoyment in what they had. As it was the friendliness was almost enough to give a substantial basis to many moments of their companionship.

They spent that day together and then the next and by that time the tension of this false position began to tell on all of them.

The burden of constant entertainment and continual peace-keeping began to exhaust Adele's good-nature, and she was beginning to occasionally show signs of impatient boredom. Mabel at first accepted eagerly enough all the entertainment offered her by Adele but gradually there came a change. Helen was constantly depressed and silent and Adele wishing to give her time to recover devoted herself constantly to Mabel's amusement. This seemed to suggest to Mabel for the first time that Adele's devotion was not only accepted but fully returned. This realisation grew steadily in her mind. She now ceased to observe Adele and instead kept constant and insistent watch on Helen. She grew irritable and almost insolent. She had never before in their triple intercourse resented Adele's presence but she began now very definitely to do so.

On the evening of their second day together Helen and Adele had a half hour's stroll alone. "Things do seem to be going badly, what's the trouble?" Adele asked. "I don't know exactly why but this summer Mabel is more jealous than ever before. It isn't only you" she hastened to explain, "it is the same with everybody in whom I am ever so slightly interested. As for you nothing can induce her to believe that you came here simply because you had never been here before and wanted to see Rome. She positively refused to read your letter to me which I wanted to show her." Adele laughed. "How you do keep it up!" she said. "What do you expect? Mabel would be a fool if she believed anything but the truth for after all I could have struggled along without Rome for another year." After a while Adele began again. "I don't want you to have me at all on your mind. I am fully able to take care of myself. If you think it will be better if I clear out I will go." "No" said Helen wearily "that would not help matters now." "I owe you so much for all that you have taught me," Adele went on earnestly "and my faith in you is now absolute. As long as you give me that nothing else counts." "You are very generous" murmured Helen. "No it's not generosity" Adele insisted "it's nothing but justice for really you do mean very much to me. You do believe that." "Yes I believe it," Helen answered.

Adele fulfilled very well the duty that devolved upon her that of keeping the whole thing moving but it was a severe strain to be always enlivening and yet always on guard. One morning she began one of her old time lively disputes with Helen who soon became roused and interested. In the midst Mabel got up and markedly left them. Helen stopped her talk. "This won't do," she said "we must be more careful," and for the rest of the day she exerted herself to cajole, flatter and soothe Mabel back to quiescence.

"Why in the name of all that is wonderful should we both

be toadying to Mabel in this fashion?" Adele said to herself disgustedly. "What is it anyway that Helen wants? If it's the convenience of owning Mabel, Jupiter, she comes high. Helen doesn't love her and if she were actuated by pure kindness and duty and she really wanted to spare her she would tell me to leave. And as for Mabel it is increasing all her native hypocrisy and underhand hatreds and selfishness and surely she is already overly endowed with these qualities. As for me the case is simple enough. I owe Mabel nothing but I want Helen and Helen wants me to do this. It certainly does come high." She was disgusted and exasperated and kept aloof from them for a while. Helen upon this grew restless. She instinctively endeavored to restimulate Adele by accidental momentary contacts, by inflections of voice and shades of manner, by all delicate charged signs such as had for some time been definitely banished between them.

"What a condemned little prostitute it is," Adele said to herself between a laugh and a groan. "I know there is no use in asking for an explanation. Like Kate Croy she would tell me 'I shall sacrifice nothing and nobody' and that's just her situation, she wants and will try for everything, and hang it all, I am so fond of her and do somehow so much believe in her that I am willing to help as far as within me lies. Besides I certainly get very much interested in the mere working of the machinery. Bah! it would be hopelessly unpleasant if it didn't have so many compensations."

The next morning she found herself in very low spirits. "I suppose the trouble with me is that I am sad with longing and sick with desire," she said to herself drearily and then went out to meet the others.

Helen on that day seemed even more than ever worn and

tired and she even admitted to not feeling very well. Adele in spite of all her efforts continued irritable and depressed. Mabel made no comments but was evidently observant. Adele's mood reacted on Helen whose eyes followed her about wearily and anxiously. "Helen" said Adele hurriedly in the shadow of a church corner. "Don't look at me like that, you utterly unnerve me and I won't be able to keep it up. I am alright, just take care of yourself."

"I wonder whether Helen has lost her old power of control or whether the difference lies in me" she said to herself later. "Perhaps it is that I have learned to read more clearly the small variations in her looks and manner. I am afraid though it isn't that. I think she is really becoming worn out. There would be no use in my going away now for then Mabel would be equally incessant as she was last summer. Now at least I can manage Helen a little time to herself by employing Mabel. Good Heavens she is certainly paying a big price for her whistle."

The situation did not improve. Helen became constantly more and more depressed and Adele found it always more and more difficult to keep it all going. She yearned over Helen with passionate tenderness but dared not express it. She recognised that nothing would be more complete evidence for Mabel than such signs of Helen's dependence, so she was compelled to content herself with brief passionate statements of love, sympathy and trust in those very occasional moments when they were alone. Helen had lost the power of quickly recovering and so even these rare moments could only be sparingly used.

One afternoon they were all three lounging in Helen's and Mabel's room taking the usual afternoon siesta. Adele was lying on the bed looking vacantly out of the window at the blue sky filled with warm sunshine. Mabel was on a couch in a darkened corner and Helen was near her sitting at a table. Adele's eyes after a while came back into the room. Helen was sitting quietly but unconsciously her eyes turned toward Adele as if looking for help and comfort.

Adele saw Mabel's eyes grow large and absorbent. They took in all of Helen's weariness, her look of longing and all the meanings of it all. The drama of the eyes was so complete that for the moment Adele lost herself in the spectacle.

Helen was not conscious that there had been any betrayal and Adele did not enlighten her. She realised that such consciousness would still farther weaken her power of control.

On the next day Mabel decided that they should leave Rome the following day and on that evening Helen and Adele managed a farewell talk.

"I suppose it would be better if we did not meet again" Adele said "but somehow I don't like the thought of that. Well anyhow I must be in Florence and in Sienna as that is the arrangement that I have made with Hortense Block, and I will let you know full particulars, and then we will let it work itself out." "Yes it's all very unhappy" answered Helen "but I suppose I would rather see you than not." Adele laughed drearily and then stood looking at her and her mind filled as always with its eternal doubt. "But you do care for me?" she broke out abruptly; "you know" she added "somehow I never can believe that since I have learned to care for you." "I don't care for you passionately any more, I am afraid you have killed all that in me as you know, but I never wanted you so much before and I have learned to trust you and depend upon you." Adele was silent, this statement hurt her more keenly than she cared to show. "Alright" she said at last "I must accept what you are able to give and even then I am hopelessly in your debt." After a while she began again almost timidly. "Must you really do for Mabel all that you are doing?" she asked. "Must you submit yourself so? I hate to speak of it to you but it does seem such a hopeless evil for you both." Helen made no reply. "I do love you very much" Adele said at last. "I know it" murmured Helen.

In the week that Adele now spent wandering alone about Rome, in spite of the insistent pain of the recent separation, she was possessed of a great serenity. She felt that now at last she and Helen had met as equals. She was no longer in the position, that she had so long resented, that of an unworthy recipient receiving a great bounty. She had proved herself capable of patience, endurance and forbearance. She had shown herself strong enough to realise power and yet be generous and all this gave her a sense of peace and contentment in the very midst of her keen sorrow and hopeless perplexity.

She abandoned herself now completely to the ugly, barren sun-burned desolation of mid-summer Rome. Her mood of loneliness and bitter sorrow mingled with a sense of recovered dignity and strength found deep contentment in the big desert spaces, in the huge ugly dignified buildings and in the great friendly church halls.

It was several weeks before they met again and in that time the exaltation of her Roman mood had worn itself out and Adele found herself restless and unhappy. She had endeavored to lose her melancholy and perplexity by endless tramping over the Luccan hills but had succeeded only in becoming more lonely sick and feverish.

Before leaving Rome she had written a note stating exactly at what time she was to be in Florence and in Sienna so that if Mabel desired and Helen were willing they might avoid her.

She came to Florence and while waiting for a friend with whom she was to walk to Sienna, she wandered disconsolately about the streets endeavoring to propitiate the gods by forcing herself to expect the worst but finding it difficult to discover what that worst would be whether a meeting or an absence.

One day she was as usual indulging in this dismal self-mockery. She went into a restaurant for lunch and there unexpectedly found Mabel and Helen. Adele gave a curt "Hullo, where did you come from?" and then sat weary and disconsolate. The others gave no sign of surprise. "Why you look badly, what's the matter with you?" Mabel asked. "Oh I am sick and I've got fever and malaise that's all. I suppose I caught a cold in the Luccan hills," Adele answered indifferently, and then she relapsed into a blank silence. They parted after lunch. "When will we see you again?" Mabel asked. "Oh I'll come around this evening after dinner for a while," answered Adele and left them.

"It's no joke," she said dismally to herself "I am a whole lot sick, and as for Helen she seems less successfully than ever to support the strain, while Mabel is apparently taking command of the situation. Well the game begins again tonight" and she went home to gather strength for it.

That evening there was neither more nor less constraint

among them than before but it was evident that in this interval the relative positions had somewhat changed. Helen had less control than ever of the situation. Adele's domination was on the wane and Mabel was becoming the controlling power.

When Adele left Helen accompanied her downstairs. She realised as Helen kissed her that they had not been as discreet as usual in their choice of position for they stood just under a bright electric light. She said nothing to Helen but as she was going home she reflected that if Mabel had the courage to attack she would this evening from her window have seen this and be able to urge it as a legitimate grievance.

All the next day Adele avoided them but in the evening she again went to their room as had been agreed.

Mabel was now quite completely in possession and Helen as completely in abeyance. Adele disregarded them both and devoted herself to the delivery of a monologue on the disadvantages of foreign residence. As she arose to leave, Helen made no movement. "The fat is on the fire sure enough," she said to herself as she left.

The next day they met in a gallery and lunched together. Mabel was insistently domineering, Helen subservient and Adele disgusted and irritable. "Isn't Helen wonderfully good-natured" Mabel said to Adele as Helen returned from obeying one of her petulant commands. Adele looked at Helen and laughed. "That isn't exactly the word I should use," she said with open scorn.

Later in the day Helen found a moment to say to Adele, "Mabel saw us the other night and we had an awful scene. She said it was quite accidentally but I don't see how that can be." "What is the use of keeping up that farce, of course

I knew all about it," Adele answered without looking at her.

The situation did not change. On the next day Helen showed an elaborate piece of antique jewelry that Mabel had just given her. Adele's eyes rested a moment on Helen and then she turned away filled with utter scorn and disgust. "Oh it's simply prostitution" she said to herself bitterly. "How a proud woman and Helen is a proud woman can yield such degrading submission and tell such abject lies for the sake of luxuries beats me. Seems to me I would rather starve or at least work for a living. Still one can't tell if one were hard driven. It's easy talking when you have everything you want and independence thrown in. I don't know if I were hard pressed I too might do it for a competence but it certainly comes high."

From now on Adele began to experience still lower depths of unhappiness. Her previous revulsions and perplexities were gentle compared to those that she now endured. Helen was growing more anxious as she saw Adele's sickness and depression increase but she dared not make any sign for Mabel was carrying things with a high hand.

On the afternoon of Adele's last day in Florence, Mabel and Helen came over to her room and while they were there Mabel left the room for a minute. Adele took Helen's hand and kissed it. "I am afraid I do still care for you" she said mournfully. "I know you do but I cannot understand why," Helen answered. "No more do I" and Adele smiled drearily, "but I simply don't seem to be able to help it. Not that I would even if I could" she hastened to add. "I am sorry I can't do more for you" Helen said, "but I find it impossible." "Oh you have no right to say that to me" Adele exclaimed

angrily. "I have made no complaint and I have asked you
for nothing and I want nothing of you except what you give
me of your need and not because of mine," and she impatiently paced the room. Before anything further could be
added Mabel had returned. Helen now looked so pale and
faint that Mabel urged her to lie down and rest. Adele roused
herself and suggested an errand to Mabel in such fashion
that a refusal would have been an open confession of espionage and this Mabel was not willing to admit and so she
departed.

Adele soothed Helen and after a bit they both wandered
to the window and stood staring blankly into the street.
"Yes" said Adele gravely and steadily "in spite of it all I
still do believe in you and do still tremendously care for
you." "I don't understand how you manage it" Helen answered. "Oh I don't mean that I find it possible to reconcile
some of the things that you do even though I remember
constantly that it is easy for those who have everything to
condemn the errors of the less fortunate." "I don't blame
your doubts" said Helen "I find it difficult to reconcile myself to my own actions, but how is it that you don't resent
more the pain I am causing you?" "Dearest" Adele broke
out vehemently "don't you see that that is why I used to be
so angry with you because of your making so much of your
endurance. There is no question of forgiveness. Pain doesn't
count. Oh it's unpleasant enough and Heaven knows I hate
and dread it but it isn't a thing to be remembered. It is only
the loss of faith, the loss of joy that count."

In that succeeding week of steady tramping, glorious sunshine, free talk and simple comradeship, Adele felt all the

cobwebs blow out of her heart and brain. While winding joyously up and down the beautiful Tuscan hills and swinging along the hot dusty roads all foulness and bitterness were burned away. She became once more the embodiment of joyous content. She realised that when Mabel and Helen arrived at Sienna it would all begin again and she resolved to take advantage of this clean interval to set herself in order. She tried to put the whole matter clearly and dispassionately before her mind.

It occurred to her now that it was perhaps some past money obligation which bound Helen to endure everything rather than force honesty into her relations with Mabel. She remembered that when she first began to know Helen she had heard something about a debt for a considerable sum of money which Helen had contracted. She remembered also that one day in Rome in answer to a statement of hers Helen had admitted that she knew Mabel was constantly growing more hypocritical and selfish but that she herself had never felt it for toward her in every respect Mabel had always been most generous.

Adele longed to ask Helen definitely whether this was the real cause of her submission but now as always she felt that Helen would not tolerate an open discussion of a practical matter.

To Adele this excuse was the only one that seemed valid for Helen's submission. For any reason except love or a debt contracted in the past such conduct was surely indefensible. There was no hope of finding out for Adele realised that she had not the courage to ask the question but in this possible explanation she found much comfort.

In the course of time Mabel and Helen arrived in Sienna

and Adele found herself torn from the peaceful contemplation of old accomplishment to encounter the turgid complexity of present difficulties. She soon lost the health and joyousness of her week of peace and sunshine and became again restless and unhappy. The situation was absolutely unchanged. Mabel was still insolent in her power and Helen still humbly obedient. Adele found this spectacle too much for patient endurance and she resolved to attempt once more to speak to Helen about it.

The arranging of reasonably long periods of privacy was now comparatively easy as it was a party of four instead of a party of three.

One evening all four went out for a walk and soon this separation was effected. "You looked pretty well when we came but now you are all worn out again" Helen said as they stood looking over the walls of the fortress at the distant lights. Adele laughed. "What do you expect under the stimulation of your society?" she said. "But you know you used to object to my disagreeably youthful contentment. You ought to be satisfied now and you certainly don't look very blooming yourself.—No things haven't improved" Adele went on with visible effort, and then it came with a burst. "Dear don't you realise what a degrading situation you are putting both yourself and Mabel in by persisting in your present course? Can't you manage to get on some sort of an honest footing? Every day you are increasing her vices and creating new ones of your own." "I don't think that's quite true" Helen said coldly "I don't think your statement is quite fair." "I think it is," Adele answered curtly. They walked home together in silence. They arrived in the room before the others. Helen came up to Adele for a minute and then broke away. "Oh if she would only be happy" she moaned. "You are wrong, you are hideously wrong!" Adele burst out furiously and left her.

For some days Adele avoided her for she could not find it in her heart to endure this last episode. The cry "if she would only be happy" rang constantly in her ears. It expressed a recognition of Mabel's preeminent claim which Adele found it impossible to tolerate. It made plain to her that after all in the supreme moment Mabel was Helen's first thought and on such a basis she found herself unwilling to carry on the situation.

Finally Helen sought her out and a partial reconciliation took place between them.

From now on it was comparatively easy for them to be alone together for as the constraint between them grew, so Mabel's civility and generosity returned. Their intercourse in these interviews consisted in impersonal talk with long intervals of oppressive silences. "Won't you speak to me?" Adele exclaimed, crushed under the weight of one of these periods. "But I cannot think of anything to say," Helen answered gently.

"It is evident enough what happened that evening in Florence" Adele said to herself after a long succession of these uncomfortable interviews. "Helen not only denied loving me but she also promised in the future not to show me any affection and now when she does and when she doesn't she is equally ashamed, so this already hopeless situation is becoming well-nigh intolerable."

Things progressed in this fashion of steadily continuous

discomfort. Helen preserved a persistent silence and Adele developed an increasing resentment toward that silence. Mabel grew always more civil and considerate and trustful. The day before their final parting Adele and Helen went together for a long walk. Their intercourse as was usual now consisted in a succession of oppressive silences.

Just as they were returning to the town Adele stopped abruptly and faced Helen. "Tell me" she said "do you really care for me any more?" "Do you suppose I would have stayed on here in Sienna if I didn't?" Helen answered angrily. "Won't you ever learn that it is facts that tell?" Adele laughed ruefully. "But you forget," she said, "that there are many facts and it isn't easy to know just what they tell." They walked on for a while and then Adele continued judicially, "No you are wrong in your theory of the whole duty of silence. I admit that I have talked too much but you on the other hand have not talked enough. You hide yourself behind your silences. I know you hate conclusions but that isn't a just attitude. Nothing is too good or holy for clear thinking and definite expression. You hate conclusions because you may be compelled to change them. You stultify yourself to any extent rather than admit that you too have been in the wrong."

"It doesn't really matter" Helen said that night of their final separation, "in what mood we part for sooner or later I know we are bound to feel together again." "I suppose so," answered Adele joylessly. Their last word was characteristic. "Good-by" said Adele "I do love you very much." "And I you" answered Helen "although I don't say so much about it."

For many weeks now there was no communication between them and Adele fought it out with her conscience her pain and her desire.

"I really hardly know what to say to you" she wrote at last. "I don't dare say what I think because I am afraid you might find that an impertinence and on the other hand I feel rather too bitterly toward you to write a simple friendly letter.

"Oh you know well enough what I want. I don't want you ever again to deny that you care for me. The thought of your doing it again takes all the sunshine out of the sky for me. Dear I almost wish sometimes that you did not trust me so completely because then I might have some influence with you for now as you know you have my faith quite absolutely and as that is to you abundantly satisfying I lose all power of coming near you."

Helen answered begging her not to destroy the effect of her patient endurance all the summer and assuring her that such conditions could not again arise.

Adele read the letter impatiently. "Hasn't she yet learned that things do happen and she isn't big enough to stave them off" she exclaimed. "Can't she see things as they are and not as she would make them if she were strong enough as she plainly isn't.

"I am afraid it comes very near being a dead-lock," she groaned dropping her head on her arms.

FINIS.

*Oct. 24, 1903.*

# THE MAKING
# OF AMERICANS

*Being the History
of a Family's Progress*

# *Chapter  I*

IT HAS ALWAYS seemed to me a rare privilege this of being
an American, a real American and yet one whose tradition
it has taken scarcely sixty years to create. We need only
realise our parents, remember our grandparents and know
ourselves and our history is complete. The old people in a
new world, the new people made out of the old that is the
story that I mean to tell for that is what really is and what I
really know.

Twenty years ago the fever to be an Anglo Saxon and a
gentleman, for why indeed should one wish to be an Anglo
Saxon if one were not to be a gentleman, twenty years ago
I say this fever had not broken over the land and sport the
royal road to this goal was still the pursuit of the scorned
few. Not that the American youth was not always accustomed to amuse himself out of doors but he did it as young
animals do because he liked it and not because of an ideal.

However the Dehnings had always had good instincts albeit these instincts sprang from peasant rather than from gentle sources and they had always hitherto spent their summers in real country but now the daughters had grown ready to be wives and it was decided that they must summer among their kind.

To whatever cause we are inclined to attribute the gentle attenuation, the thin imagination and the superficial sentiment of American landscape painting for such it is with rare exceptions to whichever one of the causes commonly urged we may be inclined to adhere there is one reason we can never adduce and that is a lack of vital quality in the landscape itself. Structure, structure, the earth has been strongly handled in the making of our prospects whether they are the concentrated stony meadows of Northern New England, the delicate subtle contours of the Connecticut hills or the rich flowing uplands of the middle South that give us an English understanding or the Spanish desert spaces of the West or the bare sun-burned foot-hills of California that make the Western sun-lover feel that to be in Tuscany is to be at home. No it is not for need of strongly-featured out of doors that we use the old world, it is for an accomplished harmony between a people and their land, for what understanding have we of the thing we tread, we the children of one generation. However let us take comfort, beginnings are important nay to our modern world almost more important than fullfilment and so we go cheerily on with our story.

The Dehning family had good instincts and even when they stayed near their kind succeeded very well in getting for themselves real country. They found for this summer a large wooden house one of those commodious double affairs with a wide porch all around standing well back from the road. In front and at the sides were pleasant lawns and trees and beyond the road were green open marshes leading down to salt water. In back of the house was a free space that opened into great meadows of stunted oaks no higher than a man's waist, great levels glistening green in the summer and brilliant red in the autumn stretching away under vast skies.

The Dehnings in the country were simple pleasant people. It was surprising how completely they shed the straining luxury and uneasy importance of their city life. Here they were a contented joyous household; the young people played tennis, bathed and rode and sometimes together with the elders they sailed and fished. In the evenings the elders played at cards while the young folks lounged and talked or danced. A number of young men and boys were connected with the family cousins and uncles who delighted in the friendly freedom of this country home rare in those days among these people and so the house was always filled with pleasant family life, an ideal background for young women ready to be wives.

The family itself was made up of the parents and four children. They were a group very satisfying to the eye prosperous and handsome; the father joyous, strong-featured and benevolent, carrying his fifty years of life with the pleasant good-nature of a cheerful boy, enjoying the success he had won, loving the struggle in which he had conquered, proud of his past and of his present worth, proud that his children could teach him things he did not know, proud of his wife who was proud of such very different things, "Oh Milly she is the girl for me" he always sang as he came to find her, never content long out of sight of his family when not engrossed by business or cards.

I said his wife was proud of very different things but that was wrong she was proud in different fashion but proud of the same things. She loved his success and the worth with which he conquered and was not far enough along the road of social progress to forget the way which he had come. She was proud too of those four children though to her thinking they could teach her little that she did not know. She was proud of her husband for himself as well as of the things that he had won though she knew that he did little things so badly and that she must be always fitting him to the place that he now held. She came toward him now with one rebuke for his song and another for his bad habit of rubbing his nose, "Don't do that Abe" she said loudly.

Mrs. Dehning was the quintessence of loud voiced good-looking prosperity. She was a fair heavy woman, fleshy but firmly compacted and hitting the ground as she walked with the same hard jerk with which she rebuked her husband's sins. She was a woman whose rasping insensibility to gentle courtesy deserved the prejudice one cherished against her but a woman to do her justice, generous and honest, one whom you might like the better the more you saw her less.

As the young family gathered about them a strong family likeness bound them to the mother's side but the deference of an affectionate reverence was for their father. To any one wise in the methods of a family progress the names of these four children ranging from the eldest Julia to the youngest Hortense through the intermediate Bertha and George would leave little for an author to explain. The eldest girl now eighteen years of age and born while the old world was

still a vital background was named from her maternal grandmother and received the Julia in unperverted transmission,
the second child though only younger by two years received
her Bertha as a modern version of the paternal grandmother's Betty. In the three years before the son was born
the first distant mutter of the breaking Anglo Saxon wave
had come to them and he was named George with a complete neglect of ancestry and only in his second name of
Simon to be slightly held as an initial was there any harking
back to sources. In three more years they had another
daughter and now there was a call for elegance as well as
foreignness and so this child like many of her generation
was named Hortense.

These variations demanded by the family progress were
accomplished completely by the mother, the father never
concerned himself in these affairs, very well content if she
was suited and always proud of her and of them all and
indeed they were a group to gratify a father's pride vigorous
good-looking, honest and respectful and with good hope of later
winning for themselves success and happiness.

And now by good fortune while our family are still standing together on the lawn an old peddler comes up the road
that leads to the house and passes back to the entrance for
the servants. I say by good fortune for so the picture is complete the picture you must understand if you are to rightly
read the story that I mean to tell.

"You children have an easy time of it nowadays" began
the father looking about him with mingled reproach and
pride, "You have to have your horses and your teachers and
your music and your tutors and all the modern improvements and yet when I wasn't any older than George here I

was already earning my living and giving myself an education. My mother too did not have a big house and servants
like your mother here," and he looked at his wife with
cheerful challenge "but Milly's the girl for me" he added
"and she deserves all she has got but as for you youngsters
I say you have not done anything yet and I am afraid with
all these modern improvements that you never will." He
paused and looked at them keenly out of his bright eyes.
"You can't tell," they answered confidently, "it will be
different but I guess we will be good for something." "No
I am afraid there is too much education business and literary
effects in all of you for you ever to amount to much" he repeated not listening to their protests, "and then you will
be always wanting more. Well in a few years we will see who
knows best for then you can show me what these modern
improvements that you think so much of are going to do
for you; in a few years I say we will see." He paused and
again looked at them keenly with the same mixture of reproach and pride and with the same side glance of cheerful
challenge toward his wife. She however had heard all this
matter disputed so often and was without interest in it from
the beginning and so she soon withdrew into the house.
The children too had heard this same story many times but
they remained for they were always glad to hear it again and
always ready to fight once more in the eternal struggle of
conscious unproved power in the young against dogmatic
pride of accomplishment in the old. "Yes your grandmother
was a wonderful woman" the father went on speaking aloud
the memories that the sight of the old peddler had roused in
him. "You are named after her Bertha but you don't any
of you look like her. She was a wonderful woman I say and

until the day of her death she could do more than all her
granddaughters put together. When we were children she
took care of us all and we were nine then, made all our
clothes and in between made peppermint candy for the little
ones to sell. I was younger than George here then and my
brother wasn't as big as little Hortense. I was only a little
chap when we came to America. We didn't all come together
and I remember how lonely Brother Sam and I were when
we left home. I remember too while we were waiting in a
big bare room for them to give us our tickets that we heard
some one mention our father's name. We didn't dare speak
to any man and indeed we didn't know which man it was but
it made us feel less lonely. Yes you youngsters have an easy
time of it nowadays I say and that was all many years ago.
Well it won't be long now before you will all have a chance
to show me what you can do for yourselves and whether all
these modern improvements and all this education business
will teach you as much as peddling through the country did
to us. In a few years now I say we will see," and the carriage
having arrived to take the elders for their daily drive the
group dispersed each to his own pleasure with a chorus from
the young ones of "Just wait and see."

# *Chapter II*

BEAR IT IN MIND my reader if indeed there be any such that
the thing I mean to write here is not a simple novel with a
plot and conversations but a record of a family progress
respectably lived and to be carefully set down and so arm
yourself with patience for you must hear more of the character of these four children before we can proceed with the
story of their lives as they one after the other grow old
enough to determine their own fortune and their own
relations.

It is my misfortune I cannot deny it, I throw myself on
the mercy of the public; I take a simple interest in family
history, I believe in middle class tradition and in honest
business methods. Middle-class, middle-class—I know that
in America we are to have none of you for bourgeois life is
sordid material unaspiring and traditional and yet I am
strong to declare even here in the heart of individualistic
America that a material middle class with its straightened

bond of family is the one thing always healthy, human, vital and from which has always sprung the best the world can know.

We need not turn Chinese though with our new-found admiration for the ways of the Far East that too may come, we need not I say believe that the only object worthy to be worshipped is the tomb of our own ancestors nor will it be found expedient in the cleanly Anglo Saxon to watch in filial piety for three years with unchanged clothing at the bed-side of an aged mother; I repeat we need not turn Chinese but till some more effective method proves itself some process more successful than any we Americans have yet discovered for remaining simple honest and affectionate I recommend you all to laud the bourgeois family life at [the] expense if need be of the individual and to keep the old world way of being born in a middle class tradition from affectionate honest parents whom you honor for those vir-tues and so come brother Americans come quickly and for your own souls' sake and listen while I tell you farther of the Dehning family.

Hortense the youngest now a little girl of ten is at this time too little to be very important to us. She was a nice little girl not very strong in health. Being the baby of the family she was much petted by the father and overawed by the brother but left by the mother more to the care of gov-ernesses than had been the case with the other children of the family for Mrs. Dehning was at this time wholly ab-sorbed by the approaching marriage of Julia the eldest and the social beginnings of Bertha the second daughter.

The boy George named under the Anglo Saxon influence bid fair to do credit to his christening. He was a fair athletic chap, cheery as his father, full of excellent intentions and elaborated purposes and though these generally were lost on their way to fulfillment you must remember he was at this time scarcely fourteen that period which has been so well called in boys the senseless age, and so do not make too much of any present weakness.

For us as well as for Mrs. Dehning the important matter in the family history at this moment is the marriage of Julia the eldest daughter. I have already told you that a strong family likeness bound all these young people to their mother's side. That fair good-looking prosperous woman had stamped her image on each of her children but with only the eldest Julia was the stamp deeper than for the fair good-looking exterior.

Julia Dehning at eighteen was a very vigorous specimen of self-satisfied domineering American girlhood. Perhaps she was born too near the old world to attain quite the completeness of crude virginity for underneath her very American face body and clothes were seen now and then flashes of passionate insight that lit up an older and a hidden tradition.

In her the mother's type had become something very completely attractive. She irradiated energy and intense enjoyment, a vigorous sprightly creature full of bright hopes and high spirits given to hearty joyous laughter and to ardent honest feeling but hitting the ground as she walked with the same hard jerk with which Mrs. Dehning rebuked her husband's sins and suggesting underneath the curves of her young face the same coarse elements of rasping discourtesy that made us fly the presence of the mother. Julia's reverence for her father's gentleness and justice and her affection for his cheery wholesome person suggested the leavening of a possible self-condemnation and a large part of our family history must be a record of her struggle to live down her mother in her.

There is an old story of a man who mercilessly and in his anger drags his father along the ground through his own orchard. "Stop," groans out the broken old man at last "Stop! I did not drag my father beyond this tree."

It is a dreary business this living down the tempers we are born with. We always begin well for in our youth there is nothing we are more intolerant of than our own sins writ large in others and so we fight them lustily in ourselves but we grow old and we begin to see that these our sins are of all known sins the really harmless ones to own nay that they add a charm to any character and so our struggle with them soon dies away.

In the eighteenth century that age of manners and of formal morals it was believed that the temper of a woman was determined by the turn of her features; later, in the beginning nineteenth, the period of inner spiritual illumination it was accepted that the features were moulded by the temper of the soul within; still later in the nineteenth century when the science of heredity had decided that everything proves something different, it was discovered that generalisations must be as complicated as the facts and the problem of interrelation was not to be so simply solved. You reader may subscribe to whichever doctrine pleases you best while I picture for you the opposition in resemblance in the Dehning sisters.

Bertha Dehning supplied for Julia her elder sister the traditional contrast. They looked very much alike these two

daughters of their mother and by strangers were often mistaken for each other, but the small thin lipped mouth in the
younger Bertha the same in type with the mother and sister
still suggested a more amiable gentleness of temper, and her
face with its oval and firm outline lacked the hard meaning
of the prominent pointed chin and the determined lines of
the other two faces. "Julia is brilliant, attractive and com-
manding but her younger sister not so striking at first sight
is of a nature deeper, finer and more efficient," agreed the
suitors and the family friends, for are we not all slaves to a
story-book tradition and can we ever think the brilliant
beauty a really good and true one and the quiet, sweet, alluring maiden the very useless member of the family. But this
is not the whole of the story either for remember reader
that I am not now to take away the character from either
one of our young friends; they may still work out the well
established tradition or they may try to prove the story-
books all wrong. Only keep in mind that futures are uncertain and be well warned in time from the vainglory of
sudden judgments.

Bertha Dehning looked up to her elder sister with family
loyalty and admiration. It was an attitude of mind common
in them all. They delighted in her freedom and her exploits.
Her father loved her energy and happiness and was very
ready to yield to her young theories and illusions, for though
he knew the value of his own experience, his was a generous
nature and he was always ready to listen to the younger
generation when they could fairly demonstrate their rights.
But the father's pride and pleasure in this girl were all ex-
ceeded by the loud-voiced satisfaction of the mother to
whom this brilliant daughter seemed the product of her

own exertions. In her it was the vanity and exultation of creation as well as of possession and she never fairly learned
how completely it was the girl who governed all the family
life and how very much of this young life was hidden from
her knowledge.

Julia Dehning at eighteen had lived through much of the
experience that prepares a girl for womanhood and marriage. I have said there were a number of young men and
boys connected with this family, uncles and cousins, generous strong considerate fellows, frank and honest in their
friendships and simple in the fashion of the elder Dehning.
With this kindred Julia had always lived as with the members of one family. These men did not supply for her the
training and experience that helps to clear the way for an
impetuous woman through a world of passions, they only
made a sane and moral background on which she in her
later life would learn to lean. With any member of this
kindred there could be in a young and ardent mind no
thought of love or marriage, nor were the sober business
men, young old and middle aged who came a great deal to
the house at all attractive to her temper ambitious both for
passion and position and with a strain of romance. No other
type of suitor had as yet appeared and Julia was all ripe
for real experience for even with her well-guarded life she
had found the sickened sense that comes with learning that
some men do wrong. Passionate tempers have greatly this
advantage of the unpassionate variety; you can never guard
them with such care but that they find themselves full up
with real experience and with the after taste of disillusion
but vitally as they are always hit, they always rise and plunge
once more while their poorly passionate fellows who receive

a vital blow never rise to faith again and only gingerly to simple friendship.

Julia as a little girl had the usual experience of governess guarded children. She was first the confidant, then the adviser and last of all arranger of the love affairs of her established guardians. Later on at a finishing school she became acquainted with that dubious character the adventurer type found in all establishments, a character eternally attractive in its mystery and daring and always able to attach unto itself the most intelligent and honest of its comrades and introduce them to queer vices. All this time too she was busily arranging and directing the life and aspirations of her family circle and she came out into the world at seventeen filled full with wisdom and experience and ready with this energy and knowledge to cope with all the world.

There is nothing more joyous than being healthful young and energetic and loving movement, sun-shine and clean air. Combine all this with owning of a horse and courage enough to ride him wildly and God is good to overflowing to his children. It is pleasant to have occasionally a sympathetic comrade on such rides. Jameson was a pleasant man of thirty five or thereabouts, a good free rider and an easy talker. Julia knew him first at home and met him usually while riding to the station to meet the daily city train. They would then either gallop home together or go about riding through the glowing meadows of low oaks, racing cheerily along the country roads and dipping here and there into a pleasant wood that broke the open country into shadow. They met too occasionally in riding parties that went in search of new country to discover and explore. It was all very pleasant and unaggressive but Julia soon began to see that Mrs. Jameson frowned in anger whenever they all met together. Then too Jameson grew gradually less comradely, more intimate and gross. Julia understood at last and did not ride with him again.

Such incidents as these are common in the lives of all young women and only are important in those intenser natures that by their understanding make each incident into a situation. Such natures suck a full experience from every act and live so much in what to others means so little for is it not all common and to be expected. In Julia Dehning all this experience had gone to make her wise in a desire for a master in the art of life and it came to pass that in Henry Hersland brought by a cousin to visit at the house she found a man who embodied her ideal in a way to make her heart beat with surprise.

# Chapter III

TO A BOURGEOIS mind that has within it a little of the fervor for diversity there can be nothing more attractive than a strain of singularity that yet keeps within the limits of conventional respectability; a singularity that is so to speak well dressed and well set up. This is the nearest approach the middle class young woman can hope to find to the indifference and distinction of the really noble. When singularity goes beyond this point the danger is apparent, the danger of being taken for the lowest of them all the simply bad or poor and from such danger the young ones in the middle class peculiarly shrink.

Singularity that is neither crazy, faddist or low class is as yet an unknown product with ourselves. It takes time to make queer people time and certainty of place and means. Custom, passion and a feel for mother earth are needed to breed vital singularity in any man and alas how poor we are in all these three.

Brother Singulars we are misplaced into a generation that knows not Joseph. We flee before the disapproval of our cousins, the courageous condescension of our friends who gallantly agree to sometimes walk the streets with us, we fly to the kindly comfort of an older world accustomed to take all manner of strange forms into its bosom and we leave our noble order to be known under such forms as that of Henry Hersland, a poor thing and hardly even then our own.

The Herslands were of the same community to which the Dehnings belonged but this family had acquired more culture in their progress. They had attained success a little earlier and had all of them by nature a pretty talent in the arts.

Hersland was well put together to impress a courageous, crude young woman ambitious both for passion and position and with a strain of romance. He was tall and well-dressed and carried himself with dignity and grace. His blonde hair which he wore parted in the middle a method of head-dress which at that time showed both courage and conviction, covered a well shaped head. His features were strongly made regular and attractive, his expression was pleasing and his manner dignified and friendly. His eyes and voice meant knowledge, feeling and a pleasant mystery.

Julia threw herself eagerly into this new acquaintance. She no longer wanted that men should bring with them the feel of out of doors for out of doors was soiled now to her sense with the grossness of the Jamesons. Hersland brought with him the world of art and things, a world to her but vaguely known. He knew that some things made by men are things of beauty and he spoke this knowledge with interest and conviction.

The time passed quickly by with all this joy of fresh experience and new faith.

Not many months from this first meeting Julia gave her answer. "Yes I do care for you" she said "and you and I will live our lives together, always learning things and doing things, good things they will be for us whatever other people may think or say."

It had been a wonderful time for Julia these few months of knowing Henry Hersland. She had often had stirring within her a longing for knowledge of made things, of works of art, of all the wonders that make a world for certain cultured people. Twenty years ago it was still the dark ages in America and lectures on art did not grow on every tongue that had tasted the salt air of the mid-Atlantic. It was a feat then to know about hill towns in Italy, we might have heard of Titian and of Rembrandt but Giorgione and Botticelli were still sacred to the few.

It was a real desire this longing for culture in Julia's breast, albeit such longing largely took the form of moral idealism the only form of culture the spare American imagination takes natural refuge in. And it was not strong meat that Hersland offered to her eager palate; still it had the flavor of the longed for dish and to her young eagerness it was plenty real enough.

The cousins and uncles who formed for Julia her sane and moral background said very little in this matter but they looked on with disapproving eyes as this new acquaintance became a chosen friend. He was not their kind and they did not trust him and men and bourgeois as they were they found his mystery no attraction.

Bertha Dehning the younger sister was not romantic

enough to feel his charm nor was she old enough to register
her disapproval. Then too it was hard for her to really think
that Julia was not more right than all the other members of
the family.

"Julia hadn't you better be a little careful how much you
encourage young Hersland," Mr. Dehning said one afternoon as he and his daughter were walking up and down the
path before the house arm in arm and in true family friendship and respect. As he made his remark he looked at his
daughter with that searching but deprecating side-glance
with which he was accustomed to challenge the dissapproval
of his wife. "Why papa?" cried Julia quickly. "I don't know
anything against him, nothing at all," began the father
mildly, "I say there is nothing against him yet for I have
looked up his record, but I don't quite like him Julia. He
comes of a family that are all successful and well-appear-
ing and I say I don't know anything against him but I don't
quite trust him. His family is alright, old Gustav Hersland
is a rich successful man who made his own money, still I
think you had better be a little careful for I don't really like
him." "Isn't that because he plays the piano and parts his
hair in the middle?" Julia asked eagerly. The father laughed.
"I don't like that very much in a man that's right, it's foolish
in a man when he is a business man but may be I am wrong
about it all, still I think you had better be careful." He
paused and once more observed her keenly with his sharp
clear eyes that were so well accustomed to judge the values
in a man.

The more one looked into the quality of Abraham Dehning's face the more one learned respect for its power and
wonder at its gentleness. It was a massive face with a firm

unaggressive jaw, loose masses in the cheeks and a strong curved nose. His eyes were blue and always bright and set between loose pouches underneath and coarse rough over-hanging brows. His strong skulled, rounded head was cov-ered with thinning greyish hair. He was a man of medium height, stocky build and sharply squared shoulders a man quick in his movements, slow in his judgments and cheerful in his temper, a man to realise and to make use of men, slow to anger and tenacious without heat or bitterness.

His children all knew the value of his judgments and the generous quality of his understanding, still he was the old generation, they the new and with all his wisdom surely he must fail to see the meaning in the unaccustomed.

"You know Julia" Dehning went on after a silent interval of walking up and down, "You know Julia that your mother doesn't like him either." "Oh mamma," Julia broke out im-patiently, "you know how mamma is. He talks about love and beauty and mamma thinks it ought to be all wedding dresses and a fine house when it isn't money and business. She would be the same about anybody that I would want."

"Yes those are your literary notions, but he is a business man and you like success and money as well as any one. You have always had everything you wanted and you don't want to get along without it now. Literary effects and mod-ern improvements are alright for women but Hersland is in business." "I know papa, that's alright but it isn't every-thing. I know how you feel about it, you think we young ones are all wrong but you say yourself how different things are nowadays from the way they used to be and surely it can't hurt a man to be interesting even if he is in business." Dehning shook his head but that head-shake carried no

conviction to his daughter and no more was said in the matter on that day.

The struggle was now well begun and Julia worked day
after day to bring her father to a slow consent. Mrs. Dehning would agree if he were willing and no one else's opinion
of the matter was important.

Time and again would Julia think that she had conquered
for her father always listened with genial amusement and
approval to the variety and fervor of the arguments that she
advanced to conquer his objections and he always openly
admired the eloquence with which she gave her theories and
convictions concerning life and business. But every afternoon as the talk came near its end in the hour that they spent
walking up and down the path before the house he would
stop and seriously observe her with his keen completed look
that was so full of its own understanding that there seemed
no room in it for any other kind of meaning and then he
would go away leaving a hasty "Well to-morrow is another
day, you think about it all and we'll talk it over by and by"
behind him.

Such resistance was hard for an impatient and eager temper to endure but they understood and admired one another
this father and his daughter and they always met again on
the next day willingly and sturdily to renew the fight.

Hersland could do nothing all this time but wait. They
were both agreed that any effort on his part to change
Abraham Dehning's opinion would make the task for Julia
even harder. It was always there that Abraham Dehning did
not like young Hersland and the noblest words nay the best
act in a distrusted person is never evidence against his condemnation. It is never facts that tell, they are the same

when they mean very different things. So Julia struggled on day after day arguing, discoursing explaining and appealing. She was always gaining ground but it was a progress like that in climbing a steep hill. For every forward movement of three feet one always slips back two, sometimes all three and often four and five and six. It was a hard long fight but the father was slowly understanding that his daughter wanted this consent enough to stand hard by it and with such conviction and with no real fact against the man such a father was bound to yield.

"When we all get home Julia you will know better how you really feel about all this," the father said one afternoon in the first weeks of the autumn that came at the end of this eventful summer the first that had been spent in nearness to their kind. "I don't say yes, I don't say no. When we all get home and are all busy and seeing lots of people you will know better what you want. I say we will talk about it all again when we get home and then if nothing new turns up and you still want him bad enough to trust to your own judgment why then we'll see what we can do, but we will leave it this way now." "Alright" agreed his daughter, "I won't see Henry any more till we get back, and I won't say another word about it all. I'll go and ride around the country and just think hard about what we have both said."

It was well-meant intention this in Julia of riding by herself about the country and thinking hard about it all but not the certain way to end for a passionate young woman her first intense emotion. The wide and glowing meadows of low oaks, the keen clear tingling autumn air, the blaze of color in the bits of woods, the freedom and the rush of rapid motion on the open roads, the joy of living in a vital world, the ecstasy of loving and of love, the intensity of feeling in the ardent young it surely was not so that she would win the sober reason that should judge of men. And now at last filled full with faith and hope and fine new joy she went back to her busy city life strong in the passion of her eager young imagining.

# Chapter IV

THE HOME THE RICH and self made merchant makes to hold his family and himself is always like the city where his fortune has been made. In London, it is like that rich and endless, dark and gloomy place, in Paris it is filled with pleasant toys, cheery and light and made of gilded decoration and white paint and in New York it is neither gloomy nor yet joyous but like a large and splendid canvas completely painted over but painted full of empty space.

The Dehning city house was of this sort. A nervous restlessness of luxury was through it all. At times the father would rebel against the unreasoning extravagance to which his family was addicted but these upraidings had not much result for the rebuke came from conviction and not from any habit of his own.

All this was twenty years ago in the dark age, before the passion for the simple line and the toned burlap on the wall and wooden panelling all classic and severe.

It was good bourgeois riches in the Dehning house, a parlor full of ornate marbles placed on yellow onyx stands, chairs gold and white of various size and shape, a delicate blue silk brocaded covering on the wall and a ceiling painted blue with angels and cupids all about, a dining room all dark and gold, a living room all rich and gold and red with built in couches, glass covered book-cases and paintings of well washed peasants of the German school and large and dressed up bedrooms all light and blue and white. Marbles and bronzes and crystal chandeliers and gas logs finished out each room. It was good bourgeois riches in this house and here it was that Julia Dehning dreamed of other worlds and here each day she grew more firm in her resolve for that free, wide and cultured life to which for her young Hersland held the key.

At last it was agreed that these two people should become engaged but not be married for a year to come and then if nothing new turned up the father would no longer interfere. And so the marriage now was made for in those bourgeois days engagement meant a marriage excepting only for the gravest cause and Henry Hersland and Julia had this time to learn each other's natures and prepare themselves for the event.

Young man if you are not of the strong men of this earth beware how you take to wife the daughter and the sister loving and loyal of simple, sane, considerate men. Her family feeling and her pure devotion to the tradition of her early home will make a test that you must needs be bravely made to pass. Be doubly warned attractive and weak brother, be sharply on your guard for it is a woman from such a family life who is so often taken by the glitter and the lightness

of your thin and eager nature, your temper selfish and demanding, but when the close life of the marriage comes, she
looks to find in you weak creature that you are the power and
support, the honesty and steady courage she has always
known and hence will spring your woe and loathsome sadness that begins and never has an end. Brother weak pleasant
selfish brother, beware.

When the twelve months were passed away no gravest
cause had come to make a reason why this marriage should
not be. Julia was twelve months older now and wiser and
through this wisdom more distrusting but always firm in
her intention to marry Henry Hersland. She loved him still
with all the strength of her crude eager passionate imagin-
ings though dimly somewhere in her head and heart was the
vague dread that comes of ignorance and a beginning wisdom, a distrust she could not seize and know but that was
always there somewhere in the background of her sense.

To her all men excepting those of an outside and unknown world and those one read about in books and men
like Jameson to whom one never could belong and whom
one always knew for what they were whenever they were
met, to her all men that could be counted as men for her
and of her world must be by nature good, strong gentle
creatures, honest and honorable and honoring. For her to
doubt such things in men was to imagine a vain thing, to
recreate her world and make a new one all from her own
head. There was the one kind one could read about and
hear of in the daily news but never could things like those
be true of the men of one's own world.

This was a thought that could not come to her to really
think and so for her the warnings of her father carried no

real truth. Of course Hersland was a good and honest man, all decent men, all men who belonged to her own kind and to whom she could by any chance belong were good and straight. They had this as they had all simple rights in a sane and simple world. Hersland had besides that he was brilliant, that he knew that there were things of beauty in this world, that he was himself in his bearing and appearance a distinguished man and then over and above all this he was so freely passionate in his fervent love.

And so the marriage now was made and Mrs. Dehning all reconciled and eager began the trousseau and the preparation of the house that the young couple were to have as wedding portion from the elder Dehnings. In dresses, hats and shoes and gloves and jewel ornaments, Julia was very ready to follow her mother in her choice and agree with her in all variety and richness of trimming and material, but in the furnishing of her own house it must be as she wished, taught as she now had been that there were things of beauty in this world and decoration should be strange and like old fashions, not be in the new. To have the older things themselves had not yet come to her to know, nor just how old was the best time that they should be. It was queer in its results this mingling of old tastes and new desire.

The mother all disgusted, half impressed sneering at these new notions to her daughter and bragging of it all to her acquaintance followed Julia about from store to store struggling to put in a little her own way but always beaten back and overborne by the eagerness of knowing and the hardness of unconsidering disregard with which her daughter met her words.

The wedding time drew quickly on through all this sharp

endeavor of making her new home just what it should be for her life to come. Julia thought more of her ideals these days than of her man and truly this man had meant to her always ideals rather than a creature to be known and loved. She had made him to herself as she was now to make her home an inharmonious unreality by bringing complicated natural tastes to the simplicities of fitness and of decoration of a self-digested older world.

I say again this was all twenty years ago before the passion for the simple line and toned green burlap on the wall and wooden panelling all classic and severe. But the moral force was making then as now in art all for the simple line, though then it had not come to be as now alas it is, that natural sense for gilding and white paint and complicated decoration in design all must be suppressed and thrust away and thus take from us all the last small hope that some day something real might spring from crudity and luxury of ornament. In those days there was still some freedom left to love elaboration in good workmanship and ornate rococoness of complication in design and all the houses of one's friends and new school rooms and settlements in slums and dining halls and city clubs had not yet taken on this modern sad resemblance to a college woman's college room.

Julia's new house was in arrangement a small edition of her mother's but here there were no bourgeois riches to be found. The parlor walls in place of light-blue silk brocade were covered with modern sombre tapestry, the ceiling all in tone, the chairs as near to good colonial as modern imitation can effect and all about dark aesthetic ornaments from China and Japan. Pictures there were none but carbon photographs closely framed in dull and wooden frames.

The dining room was without brilliancy in its aesthetic aspiration; the chairs were made after some old French fashion not very certain what and covered with dull tapestry copied without life from old designs, the room was generally all green with simple oaken woodwork underneath. The living room was a prevailing red, that certain shade of red, like that certain shade of green dull without hope the shade that so completely bodies forth the ethically aesthetic aspiration of the spare American emotion. Here were some more carbon photographs hung upon the wall sadly framed in painted wooden frames the etchings one or two of Whistler and of Seymour Haydon had not yet arrived, these were a later stage in decoration nor were there any prints upon the walls, nothing but photographs and family portraits of the elder Herslands. Built in couches and open book-cases and a fire place with really burning logs finished out the room.

These were triumphant days for Julia. Every day she led her family a new flight and they followed after agape with wonder disapproval and with pride. The mother began to lose all sense of her creation of this original and brilliant daughter and was almost ready to admit her obedience and defeat. She still resisted somewhat but was swollen visibly with admiration and with pride. The father who had always been convinced and proud even when he disapproved the opinions of his daughter, now took a solid satisfaction in the completeness of her resolution. After all to know well what one wanted and to win it for oneself by steady fighting was to him the best act that a man or woman could affect and well had his favorite daughter accomplished her end. He still shook his head at her literary notions as he called

them and at all her new-fangled ways of doing things but
he was so proud of her and of them all that his head shake
carried even less conviction than before.

Bertha Dehning was always convinced and overcome by
her brilliant elder sister though often slowly and with no
great understanding of what it was about. The boy George
admired and followed gladly with strong sympathy after his
sister's lead and the little Hortense by herself worshipped
from afar.

Altogether these last weeks were brilliant days for Julia.

But through all this pride in domination and in the admiration of her family and their friends there was always
somewhere in the background of her sense a vague uncertainty of her understanding and her right. She did not think
much in these days about the man she was to marry but she
felt him somehow in her way, an unknown force that might
attack her unawares in spite of all the wisdom and experience of her life that she felt so strongly in her mind.

A few weeks before her marriage day Julia's diffuse and
vague distrust received a sharper edge. Hersland was talking
of their life to come, their prospects and his hopes. "I've
some good schemes Julia in my head," he said "and I mean
to do big things and with a safe man like your father to back
me through I think I can." Julia somehow was startled,
"What do you mean" she said. "Why" he went on "I want
to do some things that have big money and big risks in them
and a man as well known as your father for wealth and re-
liability for a father-in-law will do all that I need. Of course
you know Julia" he added simply enough "you must not
talk to him now about such things. You are my wife now,

my own darling and you and I will live our lives together always loving and believing in the same good thing."

He said it simply enough and he was safe. Julia would not speak of such things to her father now. No torment of doubt, no certainty of misery could bring her to such dubious questioning at this late date. He was safe then, though very simply now, again and yet again he helped to make that sharp uncertainty for her more dreadful and more sure. He was in no wise different in his ways or in his talk than he had always been only she seemed to see now as dying men are said to see, clearly and freely things as they were and not as she had wished them. Face to face with nakedness in the soul of a man poorly made by God she shuddered and grew sick.

And then she would remember suddenly what she had really thought he was and then she felt, she knew, that all that former thought was truer, better judgment than this sudden sight and so she dulled her momentary clearing mind and hugged her old illusions to her breast.

"He didn't mean it like that," she said over to herself, "he couldn't mean it like that. He only meant that papa will help him along in his career and of course papa will. Oh I know he didn't really mean it like that. Anyhow I will ask him what he really meant."

She asked him then and he freely made her understand just what it was he meant. It sounded better then, a little better as he told it more at length but it left her a foreboding sense that perhaps the world had meanings in it that would be hard for her to understand and judge but now she had to think that it was all as it had a little sounded good and best. She had to think it so else how could she marry him and how could she not marry him. She had to marry him and so she had to think it so and she would think it so and did.

In a few days more the actual marrying was done and their new life together always doing things and learning things was at last begun.

# Chapter V

PASSIONATE WOMEN, those in whom emotion has the intensity of a sensation, afflict their world with agitation, excitement and unrest. Sometimes they marry well and then excitement is with them deep joy. More often their marriage is a failure and then they rush about miserable seeking to escape from misery.

The other women, those who know not passion make marriages no less unhappy but with them not to be happy makes so much less stir. They must content themselves with emptiness. They cannot overflow their misery in ceaseless restless action, they sit so quiet lest their emptiness increase and leave them with all that's inside gone and lifeless.

These are like them that have a horrid fear when standing on high places. Nothing comes to them but emptiness. They dread the loss of all themselves and every second go on losing more. The one relief there is, is to sit down and so make a resisting compact mass that will not let itself all drop away.

And so the creature without passion makes its unhappy marriage and then sits still, for what else can she do. It is not in human natures that it is still waters that run deepest. The restless ones know as keen sorrow as those who make no stir; but emptiness is more sickening long kept up than overfulness. The stomach overloaded is always very sick but then it can discharge itself upon the world. The empty starving stomach can only weaken sadden grow more help-less.

Julia Dehning had rushed upon her sorrow, passionately, fervently heroically. Bertha Dehning sank down into hers quietly, helplessly unaspiringly.

Bertha Dehning soon after Julia's marriage came to the fullness of her youthful bloom. She was darker, richer, fuller in her curves, softer to the touch, easier to be friends [with] than her more brilliant elder sister. The harshness in the speech and thought, the hardness and the jerk in the man-ner and the walk, all these her mother's ways, it had not come to her to have. She like her father loved compromise and peace. It was results that these two wanted not the strife.

Bertha Dehning was a kindly friendly creature. She liked the other girls and they liked her. Strong friendships out-side the members of the house are never the tradition of such a bourgeois family life. Julia had no such friends. Bertha a creature much more simple had certain gently tender friendships.

It was the brother of one of these girl friends who stirred in her first the hope of marriage. He was an intelligent tall efficient gentle man. His family was respected and established, longer in cultivation and greater in refinement than the Dehnings but much the same in prospects and ideals.

They pleased each other very well these two. Bertha Dehning was not a brilliant girl but her small thin-lipped mouth could pour out a very steady stream of pleasant talk. She knew the piquant rallying catchwords of the day, she was well-rounded but not a bit too fat, her face was sweetly pretty, her skin a pleasant dark, her manner gentle but with spice enough to steadily attract, the whole girl such a pleasant honest creature as to justify an ardent lover in his most fond ideals or to satisfy a prudent one in a reasoning prudent choice.

He was nice and good this lover and she was nice and good and they pleased each other very well, but alas this marriage could not be. The Dehning women were not made so simply with success to find their mate.

The elder married sister with the father and the mother often and most anxiously discussed this marriage. Surely you all know how deeply the good middle-class dread contamination and disease. This lover had a sister ill with a consumption. He had had an aunt who had died of this complaint. He himself seemed very well, but the bourgeois horror of a family taint in the father and the mother, strengthened with doctrines of predisposition and infection from the educated elder daughter, promised to be too strong for this marriage to be made.

Oh ye bourgeois! How credulous you are to all the respectable wisdom that you can obtain. All those facts and theories that their creators keep as abstract truths are for you so real so carefully to be obeyed. A little knowledge is a dangerous thing for them that have this little believe it really and use it too. Those who have much knowledge believe it, yes, but then they have too much to use for ordinary daily life and so these trust their simple instincts and convictions and always keep their knowledge only for their work.

Alas for poor Bertha and her tall and gentle lover.

It was not strong passion in these two and they were not ready for each other to do battle with all the others of their world.

Julia's dismal pictures of Bertha herself infected after her husband should develop his disease and their children cut off one by one in childhood or at birth as they were brought into the world; her father's doubtful headshake and her mother's harsh disgust, all these were too much for Bertha Dehning to withstand. Besides she herself had felt uneasy ever since she knew the facts.

She soon agreed to give it up for doubtless they were right. Her lover went away without excitement or abrupt farewell. Bertha continued to be cheerful as a pretty, wealthy marriageable girl.

The lover who came next had an easy, quick success. He was the handsomest and biggest man in the most imposing bourgeois family in their set.

This substantial family the Lohms always filled rooms very full. They blotted out all others with their solid solemn weight

# *Appendix*

### The Making of
### *The Making of Americans*
### by Donald Gallup

# 1

GERTRUDE STEIN'S monumental history of a family, *The Making of Americans,* is described on the title-page of its first edition (Paris, 1925) as having been "written 1906–1908," and its author much later referred to the book's having taken three years to write. Actually, its composition extended over an even longer period. Begun in 1903 and taken up again at Fiesole in the summer of 1906, shortly after the completion of the stories later published as *Three Lives,* it seems to have been worked at more or less continuously until the end of 1908. Then other works, notably "A Long Gay Book," "Two," "Many Many Women" and a great number of the portraits, were begun and carried along while *The Making of Americans* was still in progress, and the final section of the novel was not completed until October 1911. Ernest Hemingway was therefore more nearly correct in his statement to Ford Madox Ford in 1924 that Miss Stein had spent four and a half years in writing the book.

It began quite simply as the history of Miss Stein's own family, but it soon developed into "the history of everybody the family knew and then it became the history of every kind and of every individual human being." In *The Autobiography of Alice B. Toklas* Miss Stein goes on to describe the method of its composition:

> [Gertrude Stein] . . . always then and for many years later wrote on scraps of paper in pencil, copied it into french school note-books in ink and then often copied it over again in ink. It was in connection with these various series of scraps of paper that her elder brother once remarked, I do not know whether Gertrude has more genius than the rest of you all, that I know nothing about, but one thing I have always noticed, the rest of you paint and write and are not satisfied and throw it away or tear it up, she does not say whether she is satisfied or not, she copies it very often but she never throws away any piece of paper upon which she has written.

The scraps of paper and the preliminary notebooks in pencil and ink were never discarded and a large enough number of them are preserved in the Yale Library to bear witness to the enormous preparation which went into *The Making of Americans*. Character analyses and charts for practically the entire group of Miss Stein's relatives and acquaintances at that time were prepared in full detail, and the conclusions to which these studies enabled her to come were recorded in the pages of the long novel.

Even before the book was finished, Miss Stein had begun to look about for a prospective publisher. A draft exists of a letter sent in September 1911 to Grant Richards in England; it concludes:

> I am finishing a volume of short things and I have been doing a long book which will be done now in a few months and which I would be glad to submit to you if you are interested in my work.

Richards asked to see both the short things and the long book, and Miss Stein answered:

> I am sending you the two first installments of my long book, thinking that perhaps it will be better to have that published before making any attempt with the short things. There are four portions to the long book. I am sending you two. The third is already finished and the fourth is almost finished. I would be glad to have your opinion as soon as you could give it to me and I will send you a postal order to send it back as it makes a considerable bulk.

Richards returned the manuscript on October 17, on the grounds that he feared it would not be successful, "and we cannot therefore see our way to attempt to arrange with you for its publication when it is complete."

By the end of the month, the last section was finished and, having received no encouragement from England, Miss Stein turned to the United States. Mrs. Westmore Willcox, who was then on the staff of the *North American Review,* had read *Three Lives* for Macmillan in 1908 but had not recommended its publication by that firm. In the summer of 1911 Mrs. Willcox had visited Paris, where she had called on Gertrude Stein with a letter of introduction from Georgiana Goddard King, and had come away from 27 rue de Fleurus with a better understanding of what Miss Stein was attempting to do in her writing. Miss Stein drafted a letter to her:

> I have finished my long book and I want to know whether you

are willing to have me send it to you for your advice. Will you let me know where to send it to you. And please don't be too much frightened by its bulk. It is typewritten with wide spacing on heavy paper. I must admit though it comes to about 325000 words. Will you let me know whether you want me to send it to you.

Mrs. Willcox replied on November 9, suggesting that to avoid delay the manuscript be shipped direct to Benjamin Huebsch in New York. It was accordingly sent to Huebsch; Mrs. Willcox announced on December 7 that she had written him to be "very careful" with it; and then there was silence.

Miss Stein was not one to wait patiently for long, and her protests brought forth a report from Huebsch on March 22, 1912:

When you submitted your manuscript novel you requested that if it was not available for my list I should send it to Mrs. Willcox. I sent the book to her some time ago, but find that I failed to communicate with you. I regret the delay very much.

I find that the novel is not suited to my list, but I am glad to have had the opportunity of examining it.

Will you be good enough to send me remittance of $1.32, the amount of the charges which we had to pay upon receipt of the box containing the book?

Mrs. Willcox's answer came a week later:

I ought to have written sooner. Mr. Huebsch sent your work on to me in despair and I have not only worked over it myself but gotten several others to do so. I may be all wrong, but I do not believe that your medium will pass muster. I realize, of course, that you have something to say, but have you said it in any form that anyone else can grasp.

I am sure no American publisher will be able to cope with your book. It is too expensive a venture for too uncertain returns. . . . Your only chance of publication is in England and at your own expense. Remember that here we have the timidity of a new and young people. I note that you speak of a friend who will try to handle your mss. on this side. If you will give me her address it will probably be simpler than anything else. . . .

I thank you for sending your books to me and I am willing to believe that it is my own limitations that are at fault—but I cannot see a future for this kind of [work except in] England.

Having already had a sampling of England's reaction, Miss Stein asked Mrs. Willcox to send the manuscript to Miss Mabel Foote Weeks, then teaching English at Barnard. Miss Weeks, a Radcliffe schoolmate of Miss Stein's, had acted as her agent with *Three Lives* (1909) and had already written enthusiastically about those parts of the long book which she had seen in manuscript:

Please send me as soon as you can [*she had written on a postcard of November 21, 1909*] as much more of "The Making of Americans" as you have written. It is a great book . . . I do not think it will ever have many readers because of the repetition, but now that I feel the small increment in each repetition I am more absorbed in that than a continual wealth of new material.

On June 3, 1910, she had received an additional section of the novel, and a year later, more of it had arrived in type-script:

The manuscript came over a week ago, but I have not had time yet to do any reading. The form of it makes it so much less convenient than those blank books, though the advantage of typewriting is great. But it means that I must make a real business of getting at it and keeping the pages in proper order and cannot snatch odd moments at it. And odd moments are all I have just now. And I do find it so absorbing that there's no use turning to it with only fifteen minutes to spare.

In July 1912 Miss Weeks had still not received the complete manuscript from Mrs. Willcox, but on August 19, she reported from Nantucket that it had been delivered in New York. From there, in October, Miss Weeks wrote:

> I am reading the volumes you sent with great interest but where are Vol. III A & B. They did not come in the box that Mrs. Wilcox [*sic*] sent me and May [Knoblauch] wants the thing complete of course before she tries to do anything with it.

Vol. III, A & B were eventually located and the entire manuscript turned over to Mrs. Knoblauch, who had also had a hand in arranging for the publication of *Three Lives,* and who had been trying to place some of Miss Stein's shorter pieces with Mitchell Kennerley in New York. When Kennerley asked if she did not have something longer, she took him *The Making of Americans.* He made no decision, perhaps because there was so much material to choose from, for by this time Miss Stein herself had sent him her "Many Many Women," and he had tentatively agreed to publish that.

In April 1913 Miss Stein asked Mabel Dodge, who was at this time in New York, if she could find out Kennerley's intentions with regard to her manuscript: "There is no use in my writing to him as he does not answer." Mrs. Dodge tackled the matter with her customary energy, and on May 2, 1913, was able to report:

. . . we are now having a lawsuit with Kennerly [*sic*]. He refused to see me—talk over the telephone or anything so I have sent a lawyer who has tried to get in touch with him to ask him *when* yr book was coming out—*what* terms & to get him to give up the other mms. You see he has *all* the stuff now. An editor of the International & sub ed of Current Opinion wanted to see yr long book as he is writing an article for the Boston Transcript so I phoned Mrs. Knoblauch to know where to find it & behold—! Kennerly has that to[o]! He is holding them all for some purpose of his own. The lawyer expects today a reply from K. as he has now delivered an ultimatum. He must deliver up *all* the mms. & take or reject the *one* he wanted — & state terms. . . . I want *at once* your written authority to get possession of the Long book of Americains [*sic*]—& give that and all the short mms to a good agent here—a Miss [Flora M.] Holly that Hutch [ins Hapgood] & everybody employs. She will place the stuff if it is possible.

A little later, Kennerley had sent back six short things and had indicated his willingness to publish them. "Do you want him to hold 'Long long book' which he got from Mrs. Knoblauch?" wrote Mrs. Dodge to Miss Stein. "Now will you please write *him & me full* instructions?"

Remembering the complete lack of success which had attended her earlier dealing with Miss Holly over *Three Lives*, Miss Stein presumably asked Kennerley to send *The Making of Americans* back to Mrs. Knoblauch, who eventually returned the volumes, minus one which had been mislaid, to Miss Stein in Paris. There the war and its aftermath put an end to any idea of publishing so extensive a work, and the manuscript was stored away with the other *inédits*. An occasional article on Miss Stein reminded her public that the long work existed, however, and she later gave to Carl Van Vechten much of the credit for keeping interest in it alive through these years.

## 2

It was Mr. Van Vechten who brought up again the question of the book's publication. On August 18, 1922, Miss Stein wrote to him:

> . . . the idea of getting the Family published, that delights me more than I can say. Its a long book 2428 pages of type-writing 19 lines to the page. There is none of it in America now except loose sheets. I could send you what you liked to see of it, but as it is the only copy I have except the ms. I think I would like to send it a piece at a time to you. What do you think, should I send you the beginning and you show that and if they want more send the rest. . . . Thanks and thanks again for all your kind thoughts and may they as always bear fruit.

On April 8, 1923, she had sent the first three typewritten volumes, and on April 16, he reported their safe arrival:

> Three volumes have arrived. Please don't send any more until you hear from me. When Mary Knoblauch had the set I read a little in the first volume but now I have read it *through* and my feeling is that you have done a very big thing, probably as big as, perhaps bigger than James Joyce, Marcel Proust, or Dorothy Richardson. Knopf won't be back until the middle of May. I don't know what he'll make of it. You see the thing is so long that it will be hellishly expensive to publish, and can one expect much of a sale? I mean, to the average reader, the book will probably mean *work*. I think even the average reader will enjoy it, however, once he begins to get the rhythm,

that is so important. To me, now, it is a little like the Book of Genesis. There is something Biblical about you, Gertrude. Certainly there is something Biblical about you. I liked the passages about fat people, and washing, and religion, and old Man Hersland certainly emerges complete from this first volume.

There is another thing, the type is so dim in this copy, and there are so many errors in spelling, etc. that it is much harder reading it than it would be in print. I shall explain these things to Knopf. I wonder what he will make of it? Hope for nothing until we find out. I am sure, however, if not now, sooner or later this book will be published.

On May 14, the three volumes were with Alfred Knopf, Van Vechten's own publisher, warmly recommended. And then the only report was a montonously recurring "no news." Although Miss Stein denied on August 5 that she was impatient, she added parenthetically:

. . . I do want the Long book done and I'd rather have Knopf than anybody do it. I like the way he gets up his books. When he doesn't make up his mind does he make up his mind. Anyway accidentally one can wear something inside out and that's always good luck.

In November, she explained that the good copy of the first volume had been lost and that this was "the old and original copy when type-writing was with us in its infancy." Three months later, she had still heard nothing: "How is Knopf, any news and does he not want the other volumes they are all ready."

And now, in February 1924, Ernest Hemingway comes on to the scene. Gertrude Stein describes his entrance in *The Autobiography of Alice B. Toklas:*

One day Hemingway came in very excited about Ford Madox Ford and the Transatlantic. Ford Madox Ford had started the Transatlantic some months before . . .

We had heard that Ford was in Paris, but we had not happened to meet. Gertrude Stein had however seen copies of the Transatlantic and found it interesting but had thought nothing further about it.

Hemingway came in then very excited and said that Ford wanted something of Gertrude Stein's for the next number and he, Hemingway, wanted The Making of Americans to be run in it as a serial and he had to have the first fifty pages at once. Gertrude Stein was of course quite overcome with her excitement at this idea, but there was no copy of the manuscript except the one that we had had bound. That makes no difference, said Hemingway, I will copy it. And he and I between us did copy it and it was printed in the next number of the Transatlantic. . . .

Hemingway did it all. He copied the manuscript and corrected the proof.

Further details are contained in Hemingway's letters to Miss Stein.* On February 17, he wrote:

Ford alleges he is delighted with the stuff and is going to call on you. I told him it took you 4½ years to write it and that there were 6 volumes.

* The contents of all letters written by Ernest Hemingway and quoted in this article are copyright 1950 by Ernest Hemingway. They are reprinted here by kind permission of Mrs. Hemingway. For permission to quote from other letters I renew my acknowledgment to the late B. W. Huebsch, the late Mabel Dodge Luhan, the late Robert McAlmon, the Newberry Library, the late Alice B. Toklas, the late Carl Van Vechten, and the Yale University Library. For the use of passages from *The Autobiography of Alice B. Toklas* I am again grateful to Random House, Inc. Authorization to reprint this article was granted by the firm of Philip C. Duschnes.

He is going to publish the 1st installment in the April No. going to press the 1st part of March. He wondered if you would accept 30 francs a page (his magazine page) and I said I thought I could get you to. (*Be haughty but not too haughty.*)

I made it clear it was a remarkable scoop for his magazine obtained only through my obtaining genius. He is under the impression that you get big prices when you consent to publish. I did not give him this impression but did not discourage it. After all it is [John] Quinn's money and the stuff is worth all of their 35,000 f.

Treat him high wide and handsome. I said they could publish as much of the six volumes as they wished and that it got better and better as it went along.

It is really a scoop for them you know. They are going to have Joyce in the same number. You can't tell. The review might be a success.

The interview with Ford was apparently successful, for the first installment appeared as planned in the April number, and on March 31, Gertrude Stein received her first check— 450 francs for fifteen pages.

Meanwhile the news had of course been passed on to Carl Van Vechten in New York. On March 17, Miss Stein had written him:

I think you will be pleased that the History of the Family is starting as a serial in the Transatlantic. It begins in the April number, beginning with 15 pages and the May number will have 20 odd pages and so on. Hueffer or Ford you know Ford Maddox [*sic*] Hueffer the editor is moved he says it is magnificent and is terribly impressed with it having been done some odd 18 years ago, and as he is more or less the old guard its very good, and would it be too much trouble to ask Knopf to send back the III volume. I thought I had it all here in duplicate but that volume seems to be missing and I'll have

it copied and if he wants it again will send it back. You are
pleased with its appearing aren't you. The Transatlantic will
have to go on for a long time to do it all which may be a comfort to them and they are paying me nicely which is also a
comfort.

Van Vechten reassured her on April 13:

I am delighted to hear the news about The Family. I think
this will be an excellent way to get some public reaction to this
work and also will furnish it with a lot of splendid publicity.
I hope it will enable Knopf to make up his mind about it. I
have asked him to return Volume III to you; if it doesn't arrive within a reasonable period let me know.

Three days later a barrage of cablegrams descended upon
Mr. Van Vechten.

The first read: "Please get three volumes from Knopf at
once and hold them"; the second, "Liveright will call for
three volumes and please lend him Three Lives"; the third,
"Please take three volumes and Three Lives to Liveright
immediately."

On April 20, Miss Stein explained by letter:

That was an eruption of cablegrams wasn't it. It was this way,
the beginning of the Long book in the Transatlantic seems to
have started Liveright's representative over here and he made
me a very good proposition subject to Liveright's approval
and he wanted Liveright to see the beginning of the Long
book, and also Three Lives as the idea is to do both of them,
and he also hoped that you would see Liveright in the course
of the giving of the books which he was sure would have an
excellent effect, I more than thought so hence all those cables.
There is also some idea of your doing an introduction to the
long book, which also would please everybody.

But the high hopes did not materialize. A few weeks later, Hemingway wrote to Miss Stein:

> Youve probably seen [Harold] Stearns with the bad news. I saw him and he said Liveright had cabled he was rejecting the book.
>
> I am awfully sorry. It is such a rotten shame to get hopes about anything. I have been feeling awfully badly about it. But I will keep on plugging and it will go sooner or later. The hell of it is to do anything by mail or cable. Americans can't spend money that way. If Liveright would have been here he would have written a check, let them think it over and they will never spend anything. It is too easy not to.
>
> I feel sick about it but don't you feel bad, because you have written it and that is all that matters a damn. It is up to us, i.e. Alice Toklas, me, Hadley [Hemingway], John Hadley Nicanor and other good men to get it published. It will all come sooner or later the way you want it. This is not Christian Science.

She sadly communicated the news to Carl Van Vechten on May 25:

> There have been alarums and excursions which leave us pretty much where we were, at any rate Liveright is off, and now there is a new proposition from an English firm, anyway I am awfully grateful to you and will you get the volumes back from Liveright and keep them until the next time. Its a nuisance but then it is a long book, which will make it all the pleasanter when it comes.

The "new proposition from an English firm" was that of Jonathan Cape, who, learning of the book through Robert McAlmon, had inquired about the English rights on May 16, 1924, under the impression that Liveright had definitely

decided to publish the book in America. Cape wrote again
on the 30th:

> Can you tell me what will be the approximate length of your
> HISTORY OF AN AMERICAN FAMILY? You speak of sending me
> the MS of the first 600 pages—how many pages are there in
> addition to this 600? I would like to see this first instalment if
> you will please send it to me.

Miss Stein replied that the book would make approximately
900 printed pages and suggested that it would perhaps be as
well if Cape would look up the three numbers of the *Transatlantic* which had already appeared and see if the matter
interested him. "You also say nothing of the possibility of
simultaneous publication in America," she added, "without
which I would not care to have English publication." Nothing further appears to have come of this projected edition in
England, although there was later some question of Cape's
perhaps taking sheets of the Contact edition for sale in the
British Isles.

Carl Van Vechten eventually received from Miss Stein
the whole story of the Liveright episode:

> You see there is a man here Harold Stearns who was appar-
> ently Liveright's agent had bought things for him and accord-
> ing to him he bought the History of the Family and Three
> Lives of me. The terms were all arranged, you see I have the
> Three Lives plates and everything and it seemed an absolute
> certainly. What all happened I don't yet know except that
> Liveright cabled a refusal to him. It is a shame because there
> seems no doubt of its market because everybody likes it in the
> Transatlantique even its worst enemies say it is like Dosto-
> ievsky . . . I see that a copy of Three Lives with my signature
> is selling to-day for $13 why then Knopf should hesitate so

long, well its not for me to understand. . . . I am awfully sorry
I balled things up but it did look like a sure thing. . . . Did you
see Ford in New York he is over there gathering in moneys
for the Transatlantic. A nice man. The long book does read
well in print, I am awfully pleased and will be more pleased
well twenty years isn't so long . . .

On July 15, Van Vechten reported that Liveright had returned the two volumes, "So there is an end of that chapter.
I shall hold them until you instruct me to deliver them to
someone else."

# 3

Meanwhile the *Transatlantic* was suffering from acute
financial ill-health. Hemingway had been having trouble in
getting Miss Stein's checks for her, and in August 1924 it
looked as if the magazine might expire. The crisis passed,
however, and on the 9th, Hemingway wrote Miss Stein that
he had persuaded a well-to-do acquaintance of his, Krebs
Friend, to guarantee a sum sufficient to keep the periodical
going:

> I got Krebs to back the magazine purely on the basis that a
> good mag. printing yourself and edited by old Ford, a veteran
> of the World War, etc. should not be allowed to go hay-
> wired. . . .
> When Ford told me (the day you all left) that the next num-
> ber was in doubt and he was sending no M.S. to the printer
> in any event, I decided to hang onto your M.S. as he was
> threatening to bring out a quarterly which was pretty vapor-
> ous as he had about decided to use the death of Quinn as an
> excuse to kill off the magazine.

Jane Heap was trying to fix it up with the Criterion, Major
Elliott [*i.e.* T. S. Eliot] and Lady Rothermere's paper, and I
didn't want to have to get it away from Ford and then give it
back and gum up everything in case he did pull off a quarterly
and the Criterion didnt come through. Jane might have been
able to work it at that but the Major is not an admirer of yours
and I dont believe Rothermere could make him print it if he
didn't want to. I dont believe Jane's drag would be strong
enough to make Rothermere force a fight on the question.

At any rate now there will be regular and continuous publication and after all that is better than embalmed in the heavy,
uncut pages of Eliot's quarterly.

Soon things were again going smoothly:

I have read the proof. Ford had already read it with the MS.
Hope it will be all right. There was so much of it that he had
to set it single space but even that way it made 11 pages. I
think it gets better and better. It is the best stuff I have ever
read.

But all was still not well:

Ford, now he has a little money, is getting quite impossible. . . .
    It looks to me as though [he] . . . were preparing to quarrel
with Krebs about the first of the year and leave him holding
the bag. . . .
    M.S. received and will take it down tomorrow. The town
isnt much fun with you all gone. All the gossip dries up inside
me and poisons my enjoyment of my friends misfortunes.

There was still difficulty about getting payment for the
installments. On September 14, Hemingway wrote to Miss
Stein that he had spoken to both Ford and Friend:

Over three weeks ago both of them promised to send you your

checks for July and August and it was just yesterday, the day before rather, that I learned it hadn't been done. Krebs said they were only paying the contributors "that needed it." I bawled him out about that and told him that as far as that went you needed it exactly as much as I did and he promised to send the check yesterday. But do check up on them because it is evidently the old american game of letting a debt mount until you can regard any attempt to collect it with righteous indignation.

The only reason the magazine was saved was to publish your stuff . . . If they try to quit publishing it I will make such a row and blackmail that it will blow up the show. So take a firm tone.

. . . I corrected the proof for the October number. It is back in the regular space again, double space, and looks very good. I went over it very carefully with the manuscript. Hope it is all right.

Miss Stein followed Hemingway's suggestion and wrote to Ford on the 15th. He replied on the 18th with a letter marked "*Private*."

Hemingway when he first handed me your manuscript, gave me the impression that it was a long-short story that would run for about three numbers. It was probably my fault that I had that impression. Had I known that it was to be a long novel I should have delayed publishing it until my own serial had run out and should then have offered you a lump sum as serials are not accounted so valuable as shorter matter. I do not get paid for my own serial at all, neither does Pound for his.

Hemingway now says that you have been offered what he calls real money by the *Criterion* for the rest of *The Making of Americans* so I really do not know how to deal with the situation. Apparently your book consists of three or four novels. In that case, if the *Criterion* really is offering you real money I suppose you could let them have the second novel and rook them all that you possibly can. I should be very sorry to lose you, but I was never the one to stand in a contributor's way: indeed I really exist as a sort of half-way house between non-publishable youth and real money—a sort of green baize swing door that everyone kicks on entering and on leaving.

You might let me know your private reflections on the above in a letter marked *private*. And would you, in any case, let me know the full length of your book and its respective parts? I will then stir up the capitalist [*i.e.* Krebs Friend] to make an offer which you can compare with the *Criterion's*.

Miss Stein scrawled a draft of her reply on his letter:

I like the magazine and I like your editing. I am sincerely attached to both so suppose we go on as we are going.

On October 10, Hemingway inquired concerning this letter of Ford's:

By the way did you ever, speaking of honesty, get a letter from Ford marked private and confidential and not consequently to be revealed to me in which he said I had originally told him that the Makings was a short story and he had continued to publish it as such only to have me again tell him after six months that it was not a short story but a novel, in fact several novels? He had a number of other lies in this letter which he hoped I would not see and the gist of it was that he wanted you to make him a flat price on the first book of the novel as serials are paid at a lower rate than regular contributions like six month long short stories etc.

I don't know whether he ever sent it—if he did you might tell him you will talk it all over on your return.

I have had a constant fight to keep it on being published since Mrs. [Krebs] Friend conceived the bright idea of reducing the expenses of the magazine by trying to drop everything they would have to pay for. . . . Krebs latest idea is to have all the young writers contribute their stuff for nothing and show their loyalty to the magazine by chasing ads during the daylight hours. Ford ruined everything except of course himself, by selling the magazine to the Friends instead of taking money from them and keeping them on the outside as originally arranged. Now the two Friends feel that Krebs must show his mettle by making a Go of the magazine financially and Krebs business and financial ability and all Mrs. Krebs Friends instincts and training are that the only way to make a Go is to stop all expenditure. So I believe the magazine is going to Go to hell on or about the first of Jan and in that case I want you to get your money fairly well up to date and to have had the Makings appear regularly straight through the life of the review.

When you consider that the review was dead, that there was never going to be another number and that Ford was returning subscriptions in August (this Ford has forgotten and Krebs never knew) it is something to have it last the year out.

On November 2, Mr. Friend himself wrote to Miss Stein:

Since our conversation of a few days ago I have spoken to Mr. Ford about the payment due you for your serial which has appeared in the review. Payment has been made at full rates for several installments. At the end of December the review will owe you for five installments. May we pay, for these remaining installments, at the rate of fifteen francs to a page? If you find this proposal good and agreeable to you will you please send word to me so that I may reply with a cheque.

It is doubtful that Miss Stein found the proposal either

good or agreeable, but she accepted the reduced rate in the knowledge that it would probably be this or nothing. A little later, Friend sent payment for August, September, October, and November, and promised a check for the December number "soon." Whether Miss Stein ever received this is not apparent, for the event which Hemingway had foreseen took place, and the *Transatlantic* came to an end.

# 4

During this period Jane Heap had been continuing her efforts to get T. S. Eliot to publish *The Making* of *Americans* in the *Criterion*, but if Hemingway did indeed tell Ford that there had been an offer of "real money," his enthusiasm had led him to misrepresent the situation. Miss Heap had written to Miss Stein on September 28, 1924: "No word from Eliot—I may see [Lady] Rothermere before I go—if I do—I'll ask our fate." The answer when it came was no, and another hope faded.

But Jane Heap was eager to see what she could do with the manuscript in the United States, and Miss Stein wrote to Carl Van Vechten in October that Miss Heap was going to be "a sort of agent for me in New York," and that she might want to get the manuscript from him. "Thats alright isn't it," she added. Van Vechten replied that he approved of the plan and would be ready to turn *The Making of Americans* over to Jane Heap whenever she asked for it. This she had not done by January 20, 1925, for on that day Mr. Van Vechten received a cable from Miss Stein: "Please send two volumes Making Americans immediately publication arranged here."

The arrangement was with Robert McAlmon, who was at that time in Paris publishing under the Contact Editions imprint in association with William Bird and the Three Mountains Press. He had met Miss Stein through Mina Loy in May 1923, and was planning to publish her "Two Women" in his *Contact Collection of Contemporary Writers* (1925). Miss Stein had written him on January 14, 1925, asking him to come to see her, saying that she had something which she wanted to talk over with him. When the meeting took place, the subject of their conversation was the publication of *The Making of Americans*. McAlmon, in his autobiographical *Being Geniuses Together* (1938), recalls that Miss Stein "suggested that he publish the book in a series of four to six volumes throughout a two-year period. . . . As Miss Stein assured him that she was sure of about fifty people who would buy the book, he took it on."

On January 22, she wrote him that she thought she would like to have a contract "to affirm my property in the publishing rights of the book and the copyright, in case a volume or volumes should be all sold out and not reprinted within six months—or the Contact Company should cease to exist or fail or be sold to some one else." McAlmon agreed to draft an agreement along the lines she suggested and sent her the preliminary announcement of her book, incorporated in a leaflet listing the publications of Contact Editions.

A thorough examination of the typewritten manuscript meanwhile revealed that the book was even larger than had at first been thought. McAlmon had based his estimate of the cost of printing the book upon its size in comparison with Joyce's *Ulysses,* accepting Joyce's statement that his book contained 800,000 words. By a word-to-the-line, line-to-the-page count, McAlmon and Bird discovered that *Ulysses* actually contains only 379,000 words, while *The Making of Americans* has 550,000. "We *must* manage, somehow," he wrote to Miss Stein, "1 large, or 2 volumes. But we *must* also begin getting subscriptions to help cost." Miss Stein fell in quite readily with his proposal:

> I am pleased with your letter its hard to know how long a thing is until one has tried. Well anyway one volume would be nice and as for subscriptions I think we ought to get a fair amount fairly quickly as soon as the subscription blanks are out and these ought to be gotten out as soon as possible to follow up the first announcements we have sent out. I have sent them to Van Vechten & McBride and people in the faculty at Harvard, Chicago U. Bryn Mawr and Johns Hopkins who will all speak well of it and a number of others.

Van Vechten had meanwhile returned that part of the typescript which he had been holding, and Miss Stein had thanked him for sending it back so promptly, enclosing in her letter one of the announcements:

> I know you will like its being done almost as much as I do you have always been so wonderful about it and kept up everybody's interest in it and everything. They are doing an edition of 500 and they expect to sell it at $6, at first we thought of doing several volumes but now it has been decided, one volume of about 750 pages it would have been nice if it could have been otherwise but this will be very nice I hope.

McAlmon was soon able to report that the printer, Maurice Darantière at Dijon, who had printed *Ulysses* three years before, had started setting the type and had the copy for the prospectus:

> I put that the edition would be 300 on it, in the hopes that Cape, and Liveright will buy sheets, which they will hold till next Spring. If they don't we'll make it five hundred, and revise the slips. Later on. We insist that we are not commercial publishers. We won't be held too strictly to account in the matter of changing our minds about the size of editions.

In an undated letter, Miss Stein informed McAlmon that she had received the first proofs from Darantière "and they look very good," but she reminded him that he had still done nothing about her contract. Thus prodded, he sent her a draft, which she criticized in detail:

> The profits and the expenses which exist before paying royalties are too indefinite don't you think, it really means nothing to my end, and so I think in fairness to us all it should be stated simply that royalties are to be paid ten per cent royalties to me on the net retail price of the limited edition upon a fixed date say the first of January or the first of July of each year after the publication of the book or if it would seem safer to you say after 250 copies of the book have been sold. There should be a first payment and after that an accounting every first of January or first of July.
>
> The next paragraph should speak of sheets printed by the Contact company, in place of subsequent editions. You see the book is to remain my property and what we are dealing with are the sheets you are printing and perhaps selling. The paragraph should state, that the sheets printed should have

payed on them a royalty to me of 15 per cent by whomsoever the sheets are published a fifteen per cent royalty on the retail selling price of the book.

About changes in proof there will be no changes but it must not be forgotten that you are having no expense of proof reading as I am doing that myself.

Also will you state in the agreement that I am to have 10 authors copies free of charge as is customary.

You will bring around the right agreement right away.

McAlmon replied with two copies of the revised contract:

To secure us we have to make the figure 10%, only after 350 copies have sold, since the book barely pays for itself with the sale of 300 copies, not thinking of expenses above the printing bid we have been given. Perhaps we should charge a higher price for the book, but I'm against high prices if they can be avoided since the books just get into collectors hands, and aren't so generally read.

There is no note of the cost of proofreading, which you are doing. The last is simply to insure against long inserts and changes in the text, which I believe you do little of, but I may make a contract with other writers who do change more and maybe this will be a model contract.

Miss Stein professed herself satisfied; McAlmon came around to the rue de Fleurus, and the agreement was signed.

With this business out of the way, Miss Stein and Miss Toklas went to Belley for the summer at the Hotel Pernollet, reconciled to devoting most of their time to the correction of proof. The days there are described in *The Autobiography of Alice B. Toklas:*

We used to leave the hotel in the morning with camp chairs,

lunch and proof, and all day we struggled with the errors of French compositors. Proof had to be corrected most of it four times . . .

We used to change the scene of our labours and we found lovely spots but there were always to accompany us those endless pages of printers' errors.

During the summer, Miss Stein wrote to Sherwood Anderson:

We are here correcting proofs and getting the long book in shape, a quarter of it is already all printed and we are going on and on, it is a bit monumental and sometimes seems foolishly youthful now after 20 years but I am leaving it as it is after all it was all done then.

In August she sent Anderson a proof of the title-page and cover of the book:

It came to 925 pages and has been a pleasure to do and rather strange to do, you see I have not read it all these years. I did it just after Three Lives and I went on and on with it and I finished it, and then it was pretty hopeless and it is only recently thanks to various people among whom Hemingway counts largely as it was he who urged its being at least begun in the Transatlantic that it came up again . . . It has been printed in France and lots of people will think many strange things in it as to tenses and persons and adjectives and adverbs and divisions are due to the french compositors' errors but they are not it is quite as I worked at it and even when I tried to change it well I didn't really try but I went over it to see if it could go different and I always found myself forced back into its incorrectnesses so there they stand. There are some pretty wonderful sentences in it and we know how fond

we both are of sentences. As soon as I can get a copy of it from
the printer I will send it to you because I do want you to have
it more than anybody, well that's all there is of that.

The reading of the proof and the other incidentals went
more or less smoothly. There was some difficulty at the very
last about the return of a portion of the proofs, which, along
with other complications, delayed the actual printing of the
final section, but the finished sheets were sent out by
Darantière at the end of October and were received by Bird
in Paris during the first week of November 1925.

The five de luxe copies to be bound in vellum and eighty
sets of sheets to be bound in leather were sent to the binder,
and ten copies of the ordinary, paper-bound edition were
delivered to Miss Stein.

"The Making of Americans appeared," she wrote later
in *The Autobiography of Alice B. Toklas*, "but McAlmon
and Gertrude Stein were no longer friends." Indeed, relations between author and publisher had been very seriously
strained by various confusions and misunderstandings
which had actually begun some months before.

Even after McAlmon had decided to print *The Making
of Americans* in Paris, Miss Stein and Miss Heap had continued the search for someone to publish or distribute the
book in America. Miss Heap, in the United States, acting as
Miss Stein's "agent," was apparently not aware that Benjamin Huebsch, almost thirteen years earlier, had already
examined and refused the book. She suggested to Huebsch
in February, 1925, that he publish it, and his reply does not
indicate that he identified it with the bulky work submitted
to him in 1911.

He wrote her on March 2:

> Forgive the delay in replying to your suggestion that I ex-
> amine Miss Stein's "The Making of Americans," with a view
> to publication. I am far behind in my work and so, instead of
> postponing the matter still further as would be necessary if I
> were to read the book, I had to make my conclusion on the
> advice of a trusted reader.
>
> As I am fairly well acquainted with Miss Stein's work in its
> various periods, the reader's report confirmed my surmise as
> to the nature of the Transatlantic material.
>
> I have never been sufficiently successful in a commercial
> way to lose my delight in experimentalism, but I have never
> been far enough in advance of my fellows to be a very bold
> innovator and if I am going to be bold, I will be so only where
> my heart leads. I cannot follow Miss Stein's theories with
> enough zest to be a foster-father to her children. If her work
> had no chance to get before the public, my desire for fair
> play might prompt me to sponsor the book. But, it is before
> the public and she has no need of me.
>
> Frankly, I am far enough behind the age to prefer her
> "Three Lives" to her later method by far. . . . I wish that you
> would let Miss Stein understand that I am not unappreciative
> of her suggestion that the opportunity to publish her book be
> presented to me.

Miss Heap next tried unsuccessfully to interest the Dial
Press in purchasing sheets of the book from McAlmon. Even
the Four Seas Company, whose earlier publication of Miss
Stein's *Geography and Plays* (1922) had not been an unquali-
fied financial success, made an offer to publish an edition.
Miss Stein merely forwarded their letter to McAlmon, who
replied that it did not look very interesting: "If you wish
they can make a bid for 500 to a thousand sheets, delayed

publication till Spring 1926, but there must be payment on delivery."

It was Albert and Charles Boni who were most seriously interested over the longest period. Jane Heap was dealing principally with Albert Boni in New York and having understood from Miss Stein that McAlmon would sell sheets at one dollar per copy had no difficulty in closing an agreement to take them at "his terms." These were promptly disavowed by McAlmon, who informed Miss Heap that in order to recover his investment he would have to receive three dollars per volume for the sheets, not one dollar as Miss Stein had written her. He agreed to discuss the matter with the Boni representative in England and suggested to Miss Stein in a letter of June 9, 1925, that the Bonis might be permitted to buy up the edition, particularly in view of their more efficient distributing facilities.

The Bonis' agent did discuss the matter in London with McAlmon, who reported to Miss Stein on August 16 the firm's further proposals:

> As they can not get copyright on work set up over here, and as they must charge a higher price for the book than they wanted to, if it was a second edition after our limited one, the question came up of their buying up our edition. They can handle the distribution much better than we can, and we would fill the fifteen or so orders which are in—after the first orders none have come in for two months—and then ship all of the remainder to them, and they could bind in an American style, put on their imprint, and handle the distribution then.
>
> They would take over our contract, as it stands, and your further dealings would be with them.

Let me know if that is all right with you, at once please, so that I can go ahead and make arrangements for them to draw up a contract for you. And they may want me to tell Darantière to run 1000 instead of 500.

Miss Stein replied on August 20, from Belley:

Yes I think that is a very good idea. You did the trick in getting it printed and they can handle it as it is their business to do. You know how I feel about your having gotten it all printed so that there is this chance for it. Well you understand that. The idea then is that they make out a contract for me for the thousand as we made it for the five hundred on a ten percent royalty of the selling price and in their case bi-yearly accountings, and from them I would want a clause included concerning the date of its being put on sale in U.S.A. And also I will have ten copies of this your edition and then ten copies of their edition. I guess that's all and so go ahead and let me know about it.

McAlmon had already written her on August 21, reiterating his statement that if the Bonis took over the edition they would also take over the contract and would give her the ten author's copies called for. Her ten copies were a matter of some concern to Miss Stein, however, and she replied on August 24:

As to the ten books I want from you, you said in your last letter you were going to deliver the orders that you had had, if any books at all are gotten up in the original format I definitely want ten of them in paper cover from you for myself. That is what I mean. Will you let me know here that this is alright.

McAlmon made no mention of this point in his reply, re-

porting however that plans for increasing the run of sheets
to 1000 had miscarried. It seems that Darantière had been
blacklisted in England as a printer of obscene books because
of *Ulysses* and that mail to and from him was being held up.
McAlmon's letter to him saying that there might be 1000
had never reached him and a part of the type had already
been distributed. Miss Stein insisted upon an answer to her
question:

> . . . will you without fail answer this by return mail telling me
> definitely that if, the edition is sold to Boni brothers and you
> deliver any volume whatsoever from yourself to any purchaser
> that of that delivery I am to have 10 copies for myself. I want
> you to confirm this to me.

On September 6, McAlmon did reply:

> If Boni Bros. take over the contract they will take it over as it
> stands and you will get ten books from them, but I will have
> nothing to do about that once you've signed their contract.

The argument was never settled for on September 16, 1925,
McAlmon reported that the Bonis had "backed down."
They had, according to him, accepted by mail a price of
$2500 for 1000 copies, but when he requested a part pay-
ment on shipment and the remainder in thirty days "as·
would an American Printer had the work been set up there
. . . another partner assured me that Mr. Baer had misunderstood."

Even before the negotiations with the Boni brothers had
reached this unsatisfactory stage, Jane Heap had proposed a
new plan which she herself was sponsoring. On September
2, she reported to Miss Stein:

I have just written to Bob McAlmon making him an offer of $1000 for the sheets, contract etc. of your big book. Boni's will never take him up—the thing will hang around and lose its selling power from not being properly pushed. I'll get 3 lives reprinted as well. Will you help push this offer. I am not at liberty to tell you anything now, about who is doing this—but be sure it is none of those cowards in the "business." I'll tell you everything when I see you. God—how I have planned and worked for this—I hope it will go through.

Miss Stein had evidently seen Jane Heap when she wrote to McAlmon:

There is a syndicate which very seriously wants to put all my books on the market, Three Lives, the long book and several later and newer ones. It is for me an important opportunity. Their proposal is to buy the Making of Americans from you that is the 500 copies minus the 40 copies already ordered, for a thousand dollars which really means 1620 dollars a 1000 dollars for the 460 books and 40 ordered at 8 dollars and the five bound in vellum at $60. They would pay for the unbound sheets and covers upon delivery that is as soon as they are delivered in France.

Will you wire me your answer within 24 hours. You will realise how much this opportunity means to me.

McAlmon cabled her on September 17: "Book bound offer too low and vague," and wrote her a long letter the same day explaining the reasons for his decision: he felt that the venture which Jane Heap represented was a new one and that there was no indication it would be financed to give better publicity and distribution than Contact Editions; he suspected the indirectness of approach, which he character-ized as unbusiness-like, and wondered why the syndicate did not deal with him; furthermore, he considered the offer of one thousand dollars too low, since the cost of printing the book was over three thousand dollars, and the orders received were for the most part from bookshops to whom a forty per cent discount had to be given.

Miss Stein replied on the 18th that she did not understand his statement about expenses inasmuch as he had told her after having received the estimates from Darantière that the book would cost only about one thousand, five hundred dollars. On this point McAlmon admitted that he had made a mistake and explained that

> Darantière had sent me a bill for 51,253 francs, which had not been changed when I wrote you about the cost, 3,000 [dollars]. He had, I thought, hastily run off a 1000 on a chance that I might need them. However he had not done so and there are to be only five hundred so that the bill is reduced to 38,000.

On the 20th, Miss Stein added:

> You know perfectly well that it was not I who suggested to you selling the Contact edition. . . . when you, not I mind you, suggested selling your edition to Boni I agreed because I thought if you felt that way about it you would not sell the edition and that I did not want for obvious reasons. Even now I am afraid that after the first bound you may again not be interested and then it would be too late to sell. After all you know I want it to go big and I want to get my royalties, that is only fair. Of course my book has big publicity but that if I may [say] so is because of me. So let's see what we make of it all Tuesday and then go ahead.

To the charge of loss of interest on his part, McAlmon

pointed to the special trips to Dijon and to Paris, and the various extra costs which he had undertaken:

> . . . having done this, for a book which I did not write—much the more entertaining part of bookmaking, as printing and publishing is a grind and a drag—I don't feel like making a gift to any commercial publisher. . . . The sudden violence of interest combined with an offer that is too low from an unknown company, or one that may not yet be organized doesn't look propitious for their later disposal of the book.

On October 7, there had been still further developments. Jane Heap had turned over to Miss Stein a letter she had received from Stanley Nott in which Nott quoted McAlmon as saying that he would let the "syndicate" have the sheets. Nott proceeded to give instructions:

> Now, what you have to do is this: get the sheets, have them signed, then get in touch with Davis Turner in Paris who are my shippers in London, give them the invoice for the 400 sheets at 22? francs a sheet & the address to which they are to be sent (to me I presume) & they will do all the rest, acting on your instructions.
>
> . . . I am not used to doing business with people like [McAlmon] . . . You can deal with him better. But don't tell him so. And by the way he says that your methods are not business-like. So I leave the two of you to fight it out.

It was apparently on the basis of this letter and verbal instructions from Jane Heap that Miss Stein telephoned to Darantière in Dijon asking him to send 400 sets of sheets to Davis Turner. When Darantière wrote McAlmon for confirmation, the latter informed him in no uncertain terms that he was to take orders from no source but Contact Edi-

tions, and wrote Miss Stein that she had acted entirely
without authority. He expressed his willingness to ship up
to two hundred sets of the sheets to an address which Miss
Heap might send him. If he had not heard by the next day,
he would direct Darantière to bind the entire edition. Miss
Stein replied:

> What are you talking about. You wrote a letter to Jane Heap
> telling her you accepted her offer which letter she showed me.
> She asked me to telephone to Darantière to see if he was send-
> ing the book in accordance with the offer which in your letter
> you had accepted. Will you tell me why you changed your
> mind and when.

Before he could receive this, McAlmon had written again
on the 8th:

> Had you wished to give arbitrary orders on the book you could
> have years back had it printed yourself . . . I have a letter from
> Miss Heap which shows that she understood my letter to her,
> in which I said 200—not 400 as you told M. Darantière. She
> also understood that I felt a passing of the buck between her
> and Mr. Nott, and she knew I asked her to send ME the ad-
> dress of the Paris shipping agent. . . . That letter can scarcely
> be interpreted as giving you a basis upon which to instruct M.
> Darantière at once to send 400 sheets to Davis Turner. As
> both the cable and mail systems are in working order between
> London and Paris you could have gotten in touch with me.
>   However the book is now complete, stitched, and will be
> bound. You will get your ten copies which will be sufficient
> for your friendly gifts, and at least more than commercial
> publishers give authors. Whatever others you want you can
> have at the usual author's rate of 50% on the sale price of eight
> dollars. We will send out review copies to some special re-

viewers if you choose to send us a list of names and addresses. Further panic and insistence, and "helping" us will not delight me. Your book has had every consideration; and I have not been the one seeking to place it with other publishers. They have come to me, sicced onto me. And it does happen that I will be consulted where it is easily and courteously due me, where it is a case of my property in print. Your writing the book, does not with us, any more than it would with any publishing house, permit you to take a dictatorial attitude. Your contract was given you as your protection.

Though she was aware, as she admitted later in *The Autobiography of Alice B. Toklas,* that McAlmon's anger was "not without reason," Miss Stein had her last word:

You do forget from one letter to the next the figures you mention and you also must not forget that the communication between Dijon and London has not always been open and also my dear publisher you are not giving me ten copies even John Lane always gave the author 10 copies and mine were called for in our contract so you are doing no more than is customary but all of this is only repetition and there has been enough of that. I am inclosing the list of reviewers for you to send. Decide your 400 your 300 your 200 as you will. All I am interested in naturally as we agreed when we talked is distribution and I repeat I was requested to do as I did in accordance with your letter, one of your letters.

Nothing appears to have come of the plan for 200 sets of sheets. Miss Heap wrote Miss Stein on December 14, 1925, that Nott had ordered 200 copies sent to the shippers in Paris, but that he had had such a shock over the seizure of Gertrude Beasley's *My First Thirty Years* (also printed by

Darantière and published by McAlmon) that he could not be made to move. "We will do some publicity as soon as Nott recovers." He evidently did not recover sufficiently to do anything, and the 200 copies were apparently never shipped. The Bonis did buy 100 sets of sheets from McAlmon at a fifty per cent discount, importing, binding, and selling them at $12.50.

In December 1926 there was a rumor, reported again by Miss Heap, that "Boni's are doing your Big Book in a cheaper edition"; but this also came to nothing.

Although Miss Stein endeavored on several occasions to patch up the quarrel, McAlmon would not be conciliated. Six months after the publication of the book, he sent her an ultimatum:

> Contrary to your verbal statements that you would help rid us of your volume, you have done nothing. The Dial review I got for you. The Irish Statesman review, came from a book sent them at my instructions. Books were sent to people you asked to have them sent to. Ten books were given GIVEN you. You *asked* me to take on the book. You knew it was a philanthropic enterprise as the Ms. had been some twenty years on your hands. There is no evidence of any order having come in through your offices except from your immediate family . . . the family, one judges, mentioned in the book. . . .
>
>     If you wish to purchase the rest of the books you may do so. . . . As the Three Mts. Press is now non-existant, and any publishing I do will be as a private person, using the name Contact, and as Mr. Bird is out of it, I do not choose to bother storing a book of that size, when its author so warily fears we might get back a portion of the amount paid for it.
>
>     . . . If you wish the books retained, you may bid for them.

Otherwise, by Sept.—one year after publication—I shall simply rid myself of them en-masse, by the pulping proposition.

As McAlmon observed, the book had not received much immediate publicity. Marianne Moore, in the *Dial* review referred to by McAlmon, compared it to *Pilgrim's Progress:*

As Bunyan's Christian is English yet universal, this sober, tender-hearted, very searching history of a family's progress, comprehends in its picture of life which is distinctively American, a psychology which is universal.

Edmund Wilson reviewed it in the *New Republic,* but admitted to not having read it through:

I do not know whether it is possible to do so. . . . With sentences so regularly rhythmical, so needlessly prolix, so many times repeated and ending so often with present participles, the reader is all too soon in a state, not to follow the slow becoming of life, but simply to fall asleep.

The *Irish Statesman,* asserting that "it must be among the seven longest books in the world," attempted to review the book "in a manner resembling that in which it is written":

There is serious thinking and nice picturing of being living, but certainly we were sometimes feeling that anyone might be writing like this if they were abandoning their being to it.

William Rose Benét headed his comment in the *Saturday Review of Literature* "We Cease Being Living," and summarized his conclusions:

[Miss Stein] has accomplished the most perfect imitation of the conversation that went on in that tall tower on the plain

of Shinar that I could possibly have imagined. She has ex-
hibited the most complete befuddlement of the human mind.

The reviews, except for Marianne Moore's, did little to
stimulate sales of the book. Through the end of December
1926, one de luxe, 28 leather, and 74 paper-bound copies
had been sold and paid for. The 5 de luxe copies had been
received from the binder on February 22, 1926, and the
question of Miss Stein's signing them had resulted in another little tiff, this time with William Bird. She refused to
sign those which had not actually been sold, and Bird, who
had been sick, replied on March 5:

> I do not see why you should sign any at all. Nor do I see why
> I should be bothered five times about this matter.

On September 18, 1926, Jane Heap had written Miss
Stein:

> I have seen Bob [McAlmon] several times . . . When I talked
> to him about the book he . . . said he knew nothing about it.
> I called to see Bird but he was away for a few days. I had a
> short talk with Sylvia [Beach]. Bob has told her that you are
> cheating him or trying to cheat him—I won't talk to her again
> until I have seen Bird with the proposition about the con-
> tract—Tomorrow I hope.

Nothing apparently came of this. Gertrude Stein never
bought the remaining copies from McAlmon, nor did he go
to the expense of having them pulped as he had threatened
to do. The business difficulties with the Bonis were repeated
in the case of other American firms. A few copies were sent

out now and then to bookstores, but it was not easy to collect payment for them. Mr. McAlmon states that certainly not over 200 copies were distributed in this way and only perhaps five per cent of those were ever actually paid for. What became of the remainder of the edition neither McAlmon nor Bird remembers, but it is certain that a relatively small number of copies actually reached the hands of readers.

Its post-publication history sheds a good deal of light on the lack of success which *The Making of Americans* suffered. But although Miss Stein was disappointed in her hope for royalties from the sale of McAlmon's edition, and the initial distribution of the book was so restricted, its reputation grew gradually over the following years. In 1929, selected passages amounting to about sixty pages of the English text were translated by Georges Hugnet with Miss Stein's assistance and printed in Paris. A condensation planned for American publication to make about four hundred pages actually appeared first in a French translation by Bernard Faÿ and the Baroness Seillière in Paris in 1933; it was eventually published in the United States by Harcourt, Brace in 1934 as a result of the interest in Miss Stein's earlier work stimulated by the success of *The Autobiography of Alice B. Toklas* (1933). Bad luck continued to haunt the book, for three days after the contract for this abridged edition was signed with Harcourt, Brace, Bennett Cerf cabled asking to do it complete in the Modern Library Giants. This shortened version was allowed to stay out of print until 1965, when a paperbound edition was issued by Harcourt, Brace & Howe in their series of Vintage Books. In the same year an unauthorized offset reprint of the complete text was issued in New York by the Something Else Press. As with her first published work, *Three Lives*, the reception by the public of *The Making of Americans* must have been a bitter disappointment to Miss Stein. Its publication could hardly have been attended by more numerous and varied misfortunes, continued over a greater number of years.